A SPARKLING CHRISTMAS MOSCATO

ANNA REZES

ISBN: 978-1-950657-21-6 (paperback)

ISBN: 978-1-950657-20-9 (ebook)

This is a work of fiction. Names, characters, places, and incidents are either a product of the author's imagination or are used fictitiously. Any resemblance to actual persons, living or dead, events, or locales is entirely coincidental.

Cover design by German Creative

First Edition: 2020

Words Imagined

Hilliard, OH

www.annarezes.com

This is as close to Hallmark as I get.
Fucking deal with it!

MILLIONS OF DAZZLING LIGHTS

WILLA

INSIDE, it was cozy and warm with a backdrop of familial contentment. The din of football coming from the television was a comforting sound that I'd grown to associate with the holidays. My mom was crocheting a blanket while my dad and Oliver made predictions about which teams would make it to the Super Bowl. My mom piped up and told them they were both wrong, making her own educated guess.

This weird sense of normalcy settled over me, lulling me to sleep. Well, that and I had overstuffed myself with second helpings from our Thanksgiving feast. It was hardly my fault that I had practically put myself into a food coma. My parents loved to cook and prided themselves on the recipes they'd perfected over the years.

I was happy.

No. Happy was undercutting all that I felt. It was a bone-deep comfortable kind of happy, like a restful sigh settling over my soul. I hadn't felt this at peace since I was very young. Joy danced inside me like a carefree child, until a sharp, unsettling feeling overtook it. The damaged part of me—the divorced, bitter, disillusioned part—scolded my inner joy for being so childish.

This could all be temporary.

That's when I left the comfort and warmth of inside to get some fresh air and hopefully subside my panic. I wanted to keep this happy, safe feeling. But knowing it could all be taken away scared the daylights out of me.

The crisp air had me pulling my sweater tighter around myself. I stood on my parents' wraparound porch, looking out over the field behind their house. I missed the warm orange and yellow hues of October. The end of November in Kentucky brought frost and death, turning everything the same shade of lifeless grey-brown.

A shiver rattled me, and I wished I thought to grab my coat, but I wasn't planning to stay out here for much longer. I heard the door open behind me, and then there were footsteps on the worn floorboards. Oliver draped my coat over my shoulders and wrapped his arms around me. He stood a whole head taller than me and I felt small in his arms. He was handsome with dark hair and olive skin. His hair was long enough for a man bun when we'd met, and as much as I liked the wild unkempt Oliver, he was just as handsome with his hair short and clean cut. The little stubble on his cheeks was proof he hadn't shaved today. I loved that he was comfortable enough around my family that he could be his laid-back self.

"You okay?" His breath fell against my ear, and I felt goosebumps spread.

"I feel like I can't trust this." I spun in his arms to face him. "All the warm, happy feelings gushing through me feel so fragile. I never knew what blissfully happy was, and now that I do, I'm terrified it's going to fall apart."

His striking blue eyes held so much emotion. "Willa, I'm not going anywhere. This is our year of firsts. We had our first Halloween and Thanksgiving together, and we still have Christmas and New Year's Eve, among others. Just try to stay in the moment with me."

I wrapped my arms around him, and he returned my embrace. I felt a sense of calm and peace. The beginning of our relationship had been messy, but he'd more than made up for it. He buried his face in my nearly black waves, and I savored the tender moment.

We had both gotten out of long-term relationships, and we were trying to take things slow, but he'd moved states to be with me. He'd rented an apartment but spent most of his free time at my house. He had more than a drawer in my dresser. He had two and some space in my closet. It was a prolonged move-in process that we never really talked about.

"I'm nervous about going to your parents' for Christmas. What if they hate me?"

"Willa, you're unhateable."

I laughed. "And you're full of shit."

He pulled me closer. "Seriously, they'll love you. They're just shaken up over Addison and me breaking up."

"You mean, getting divorced."

"Sure, if you wanna get technical."

Oliver had been married for a day before he and Addison started the divorce process. Between her affair and him falling in love with me, they realized getting married was the wrong decision. They could have gotten an annulment, but the process took longer than a divorce, and Oliver was in a hurry to win me back.

Their marriage was short but their relationship spanned over a decade, and their families had been shocked at the news of them splitting up. The two of them hadn't given details to what led to the breakup, saying it was no one's business. But when Oliver's family learned he was moving out of state to be closer to his new girlfriend, they weren't happy.

Looking at it from the outside, I probably wouldn't like me in this situation either, especially because Addison was pregnant with Oliver's child. She'd secretly been two months along when they'd said their wedding vows.

Addison had moved with Oliver—different houses, same city—and was supportive of our relationship, which made for a weird dynamic. We were friendly, but I wouldn't call her my friend.

I didn't want to know what Oliver's family thought about me, but we would find out soon enough as we were headed to see them next month.

The back door opened, and Bella shot out the door, running out into the yard to sniff around and do her business. She was a boxer, blue heeler mix I'd had since she was a puppy.

Oliver squeezed me. "Don't worry, Willa. They know what happened between Addison and me isn't your fault. I want you to meet them."

"I want to meet them too. I just want them to love me as much as my parents love you. And I'm afraid that's not possible." I looked out over the yard as Bella joined us on the porch, and to change the subject, I added, "Everything is so grey and gross out here. I can't wait to get home and begin decorating. Give some color back to this gloomy season."

Oliver raised his brow. "How much decorating are we talking?"

"I got rid of a lot of stuff, but there are still several totes in the garage."

He sighed, and I added, "At least I'm not one of those crazy people who put their Christmas tree up the day after Halloween."

He laughed. "Come on, Willa. Let's go inside."

WHEN WE MADE it back to my house, we parked on the side, by the detached garage, and I walked to the front of the house, looking it over to get an idea of how I planned to decorate. I loved my cozy cap cod. It was much smaller than the McMansion I'd lived in with my ex, but I always disliked that house. It was too big for the two of us, and financially, it left us barely scraping by. I hated being house poor.

Oliver followed me, asking, "Why don't I take you to get a real tree?"

I laughed. "I have an artificial tree, which is much easier."

"Yeah, but where's the fun in that? Come on. Don't you want the whole Christmas experience?"

I shrugged. "The last time I got a real tree, it died, and I had to throw it out before Christmas."

"Well, if this one dies, I'll go get another one."

"But then we'd have to decorate it all over again and redo the lights, and Bella is bound to destroy it."

"Are you always so practical?"

"No, but I am about this. You've played fetch with Bella. You throw a twig, and she comes trotting back with an entire branch. I can't imagine what she'd do if I brought a real tree into the house."

Oliver noted my horror and conceded. "You might have a point."

"Besides," I said, moving toward the detached garage. "The artificial tree has the lights attached, and there's no water in the tree stand for Bella to get into."

"Do we have any guarantee she'll leave the artificial tree alone?"

"She has in the past. We just can't have any ornaments on the bottom. But she was only a year old last Christmas, so she might do better this year."

Oliver helped me pull several large totes of decorations from the high shelves in the garage. I was excited about Christmas with Oliver this year. Last year, my marriage was falling apart. I'd known about the affair, but I pretended everything was fine. I wasn't ready to deal with it, but I walked in on them together a few days before Christmas. It made for a very depressing holiday.

CHRISTMAS MUSIC WAS HUMMING ABOUT silent nights in the background while we unpacked the holiday decor. I'd purchased pine-scented candles for this very occasion, and my cozy living room was already beginning to feel festive. While I sat on the floor pulling decorations out of the bins, Oliver kneeled, laying out all the spools of neatly wound

Christmas lights. Once he had them all out, he paused, gawking at them. "Everything is so organized," he commented, holding up a spool and pointing to the label. "I mean, you actually labeled each of these."

I pride myself on my organization skills and could barely keep the satisfied grin off my face. "It might take more time to put things away, but it makes it so much easier to know what's what when unpacking things. And things fit in the bins better this way. I swear, having everything in order makes decorating more fun."

Oliver grinned and pulled me forward to kiss my forehead. "You're cute when you nerd out. I bet you love The Container Store."

I shifted my eyes to the side. "Mayyybe, among others."

He chuckled, sitting on the floor across from the bin I was unpacking.

Running my fingers along the garland I pulled from the bin, I said, "I can't imagine Addison is unorganized."

"No, but her organization isn't on this level." He waved at our surroundings.

I raised my brows. "And what level is that?"

"Uhh . . ." His eyes shifted. "I think there's another game on TV."

"Nice topic change. Real subtle." I shook my head. "Did you used to help Addie decorate for Christmas?"

"Yeah, but we kept things pretty simple. She was always busy, and as long as we had a tree, I didn't really care about the rest of it."

"This will be the easiest decorating of your life thanks to my *level of organization*, and I already have ninety percent of my Christmas shopping done."

"You've already bought gifts?"

"Of course. I usually start in October." He gawked at me, and I went on. "I like to plan ahead."

He sighed. "So, do you know where you're putting all this stuff?"

I pulled out a boxwood wreath. "Not exactly. But I have an idea. Next year will be even easier." I looked at him. "Don't you have Christmas decorations of your own, or did Addie keep everything?"

"Addison has them all."

"Do you want any of them?"

He shrugged. "She's going to go through them when she puts up her stuff. I don't really have anything I'm particularly sentimental about."

"Really?" I had a hard time believing there was nothing he wanted. "I have a lot of sentimental things."

"So does Addison, which is why I left it to her. What's your most sentimental Christmas decoration?"

"Probably my grinch doll from when I was a kid. It's super ugly, but I love it. I'll put it on my bed with all the throw pillow you hate."

"I don't hate them. They just don't serve any purpose."

"Their purpose is to be pretty and soft and feminine. It's like jewelry for my bed."

"But we're the only ones who see it."

"I don't do it for other people. I do it for me. It makes me happy, just like my ugly grinch doll. Prepare to embrace its ugliness."

He laughed. "I should've known your favorite thing about Christmas was the grinch."

I shrugged. "It could be worse. My grandpa used to have

this two-foot-tall spinning nutcracker that played music. It was my favorite thing to play with when I was little, and after he died, my parents kept it. They put the ugly thing out every year because they knew it reminded me of Christmases with my grandpa. But we lost it when our house caught fire when I was twelve. We were lucky the fire wasn't worse, but I remember being so upset about losing that stupid nutcracker."

"Have you looked for another one?"

"Yeah, but it was an old toy from the sixties that no one remembers, let alone kept. It wasn't a big deal. My parents found something similar, and I've pretended to love it, but it's not the same."

He frowned, and I put the wreath aside to pull out a wooden box filled with bows.

"Hmm . . ." Oliver had his hand up to his chin, his index finger pressed to his lips and a distant look on his face. "I guess I have a glass cookie ornament from Gran." He dropped his hand and looked at me. "I really wish you could've met her. You would've loved her. She was a firecracker inside this tiny little body. I made cookies with her every year, and I'm not one to bake a lot, but I still make those cookies. I think of her every single time. She gave me the cookie ornament one year as a way to commemorate our tradition."

I leaned forward and poked him in the shoulder. "See, I knew there was a softy in there under all those layers of hard male."

His eyes narrowed, and he shoved the bin that separated us off to the side. He crawled toward me. "I'll show you a hard male."

I squealed and scooted back, but I wasn't quick enough. He caught my foot and pulled me toward him until I was lying on my back, and he was crawling over me. His lips fell on mine, and I wrapped my arms around him.

Then Bella was licking the side of our faces, and Oliver snickered against my lips. "Damn."

"It was a good thought," I said when he pulled back. Bella continued to wiggle and bounce, thinking we were on the floor to play. She was jumping all over the things we'd laid out on the floor. Oliver sat up, moving to contain her while I tried to pull things back in order.

THE DAYS GREW SHORTER. The afternoon light bled from the sky, and darkness crept in, making it feel like nighttime before most people were even off work. I had the constant urge to hibernate. I wanted to spend the entire winter locked in the house with Oliver and Bella, eating spicy chili and warm sugar cookies fresh from the oven. Bella was on board, but neither Oliver nor my best friend, Jodi, would allow that. Oliver always had his hands in something. He wasn't one to veg. And Jodi would break down my door and drag me out of the house if I went more than a week without seeing her. She lived only a couple of doors down from me and often pulled me out to do random errands with her, which is precisely what she did today. She dragged my ass out into the freezing cold so I could help her with her Christmas shopping.

We had already been in and out of five stores when twilight invaded. As the sky darkened, the shopping center came to life, lighting up like a winter wonderland. Over the stone paths between shops were millions of dazzling lights strung up, making it feel like Christmas. The jingling of bells got louder as we walked. It was such a festive sound that grew increasingly louder. I felt like I was about to meet Santa's reindeer. Then I heard the clopping of hooves before the majestic white horse came into view. The bells hung around its neck while it pulled the glitzy Christmas carriage behind it. We stopped to watch, noticing the line of people down the block. They were all waiting for a carriage ride. The horse trotted past us, the bells so loud I couldn't think, and I suddenly felt bad for the poor horse having to listen to that racket all day.

As we walked into another shop, Jodi said, "I should be a good mom and bring my kids here to do the Elf scavenger hunt."

"The what?"

She pointed to an elf doll posed to look like he was stealing Christmas lights off of a tree in the window display. "A bunch of these shops have those elf dolls doing all kinds of stupid things. It's fun for the kids to go around and see if they can find them all. They get so excited. It's kinda cute. Okay, I'm definitely bringing those hellions back here."

"What fun."

She looked at me. "You wanna come? We could bring flasks and make it a drinking game."

"You wanna get drunk at a shopping center while you have all your kids with you?"

"I'll bring James. He'll be the responsible parent for the evening."

"Jodi, I love you, but I might skip that one."

"Okay. There's an ugly sweater bar crawl on the

sixteenth. You wanna go with me? The kids are staying with James' parents so we can stay out as late as we want."

"I thought motherhood was supposed to tame you."

"No, it just suppresses my inner wild woman until I can't stand it any longer and sucker James' parents into watching them so momma can escape and be crazy for a night."

No one could say I half-assed things. My shaggy green sweater looked like a pine tree. It was wrapped in garland and twinkling lights. I hid the battery pack for the lights in the pocket of my jeans. Multicolored ornaments hung off the sweater, and when I pressed a button, they sang Christmas carols. It was elaborate, but when I agreed to the Ugly Sweater Bar Crawl, it meant I was fully committed.

Oliver's blue sweater had a fuzzy white abominable snowman that took up the entire front. He still looked sexy in the ridiculous sweater. We were on our third stop, and I was already encouraging Jodi to drink water. Her husband went to fetch a glass while Jodi leaned into me at our bar-top table.

"I miss ma kids," she slurred sloppily. "Can I haff one adult night without thinking bout 'em." She shook her head. "Nope. Cuz they're the best little assholes, and I luv em."

I put my arm around her so she didn't fall off her chair. "I know you do, Jodi."

She looked up at me. "Cow weigh tazee you azza mum."

"You can't wait to see me as a mom?" I clarified.

She nodded.

"I know, but I get to spoil your kids."

"Those bastards're lucky to've Aunt Wilwa in'er lives."

James came back with water. "Here, baby. Let's take a sip." He peeled her off me, and Oliver swept in from somewhere. I'd lost track of him.

"Hey, Willa, it's our turn."

Had I missed something? "Our turn for what?"

He gave me a goofy smile and pulled me off my chair, wrapping his arm around my shoulder. I'd forgotten how playful Oliver was when he was drunk.

As he guided me through the throngs of ugly sweaters, I asked, "Where are you taking me?"

He didn't answer, but it didn't take long to notice he was leading me toward the stage. With great dread, I said, "Karaoke?"

He gave me his goofiest grin and nodded. "It'll be fun."

"Did you pick a song?"

"Yeah, but it's not a duet so you don't even have to sing if you don't want to."

I narrowed my eyes at him, giving him my dirtiest look.

He grinned. "I dare you."

I sighed. "I should've seen that coming." He knew I wouldn't back down if he dared me to do something. It was an ongoing competition, and I wasn't about to lose.

"So, you'll do it?"

"Of course, but payback's a bitch."

He smiled at me as we climbed on stage. From the other side of the room, I heard Jodi cheering us on. There were two mics set up next to each other, and Oli took one while I took the other. I'd just gotten it adjusted to my height when the music started playing. I laughed, shooting Oliver a grin, and then looked at the word prompter as the first words lit up the screen.

YOU'RE A MEAN ONE
MR. GRINCH
YOU REALLY ARE A HEEL

Everyone in the bar was drunk, and I'd already decided life was more fun when we stopped caring so much about what people thought of us, so I sang my heart out. I didn't need the prompter. I had this song memorized.

By the time we got to the *Stink Stank Stunk,* I was pinching my nose and singing directly to Oliver as if the song was about him. He was singing it back to me, and maybe it was the booze, but we didn't sound so bad.

When we got to the end, we bowed to the crowd.

"Encore!" Jodi shouted from the back.

I grabbed Oliver's hand and hauled him off stage before the crowd got it in their head to join Jodi in her "encore" chant.

"We have one more bar, but I think Jodi's spent," I said.

"Do you think she could do the photo booth?"

"There's a photo booth?"

"At the next place, there is."

"Okay, maybe we can carry Jodi there. We need a photo to commemorate this beautiful night."

James was as reserved as Jodi was outgoing. He didn't talk much, but that was okay because Jodi could carry the conversation all by herself. When I'd first met him, I didn't immediately like him. It wasn't until he came to pick up a drunk Jodi from my dorm room years before that I realized he was a great guy. The way he treated her with so much care and patience was adorable and melted my heart. When

Jodi wasn't around, he could be somewhat talkative. And he was a really intelligent guy. He'd definitely be the one helping their kids with their future math homework.

James gave Jodi a piggyback ride to the bar next door, and we took some great photos with all the holiday-themed props.

BEACHED WHALE

OLIVER

BELLA BARKED when someone pulled into the driveway. I stood to peek out the window.

Willa's school had already let out for holiday break, so she was sitting on the living room floor wrapping gifts. "Who's here?"

"Addison," I said as I walked into the kitchen. "She's early."

The door off the kitchen opened to the driveway. I stepped out the back door as Addison was opening her trunk.

"You're early," I said, walking to her.

She glanced at me. "Yeah, I went through our Christmas stuff and have a box of your things." She reached in the trunk, groaning as her belly got in the way. Her baby bump strained against the seams of her parka, preventing her from bending like she used to.

I reached in and grabbed the box.

"Thanks," she said on a sigh. She closed the trunk and followed me to the back door.

"How are you feeling?" I asked as I balanced the box against my side to free a hand so I could open the door for her.

She rolled her eyes as she walked past me through the door. "Certainly not like a beached whale."

"I'm sensing some sarcasm," I said, following her inside.

She set her purse down on the kitchen table and stripped out of her coat. "Why did I even wear this thing? Pregnancy has essentially turned me into a furnace."

I closed the door behind us and said, "It's only twenty degrees today."

The static from her coat had her long blonde hair standing on end. She ran her fingers through it, trying to tame it. And then gave up and tucked it behind her ears. Her fair skin flushed from the heat, and her blue eyes narrowed on me as she put her hands on her hips. "What's your point?"

Abort, abort. "You do what makes you most comfortable."

"Comfortable? Ha. I'm almost eight months pregnant. There is no such thing as comfortable anymore."

"Well, you look nice." Addison was always put together. Pre-pregnancy, she had a modelesque figure, tall and thin. She carried what little pregnancy weight she'd gained in her belly, but she wasn't used to having a less than perfect physique, so pregnancy hadn't been easy for her.

"Hey, Addison," Willa said, joining us in the kitchen.

Addison looked at her. "I didn't know you'd be home."

"My school starts the holiday break early. Perks of being a teacher."

Addison let out a long breath. "That sounds nice. I could use a few weeks off. Are you going with us to the doctor?"

Willa shook her head. "No. I would never intrude like that. It's your appointment. It should be the two of you. But I am excited to see the ultrasound pics."

I wrapped my arm around Willa's shoulder, grateful to be with someone so understanding. She'd been amazing through this whole situation, and I was lucky she'd given me a second chance.

Willa changed the subject, pointing to the box I'd placed on the counter. "So are those Oliver's ornaments?"

Addison took a step forward, opening the flaps. "Yeah, ornaments and a few other things. I know you said you only cared about the ornaments, but I thought you'd want this." She pulled out a laminated recipe card with a Rudolph cardholder.

"My grandma's recipe." I stepped forward to take it from her. "I can't believe I forgot about this. I even told Willa how I made my grandma's cookies every year."

Addison peeked at Willa, saying, "They're delicious."

Willa said, "Can't wait to try them. And to be honest, I'm excited to watch him bake something."

Addie smiled, admitting, "I made a copy of the recipe before bringing it here."

"They aren't vegan," I noted.

With a hint of attitude, Addie said, "I feel like pregnancy is a good enough reason to splurge sometimes." She smiled and patted the box. "Do you want to go through the rest of the box now?"

I shook my head. "No, I'll go through it later."

Addison looked to Willa and asked, "Would you want to go to a wreath workshop with me?"

"Umm. Sure. When is it?"

"Next Tuesday evening. The twenty-second."

"That's the day we're leaving for New York."

"Oh, I didn't realize you were going that early." She seemed uncomfortable. "Well then, never mind."

Willa asked, "Are there any other workshops?"

"Yes, but I'm working and can't make any other times. I guess we'll see each other in New York."

I looked at Willa. We exchanged a tiny conversation with a meaningful glance before I turned back to Addison. "Would you want to ride with us to New York?"

She shook her head. "Thanks for the offer, but I have plans to pick up Travis so he can make the trip with me."

I still hadn't acclimated to Travis being only a few hours away. I nodded, looking at the clock. "Do you want to go now? We should have time to stop at the vegan bakery before the appointment."

"Sure."

"Do you want me to drive?"

"I'm perfectly capable of driving," she snapped.

I put my hands up in surrender. "I know. Just asking. Let's go."

While she grabbed her things from the table, I grabbed my coat and kissed Willa.

"Bye, Willa," Addison called, sounding much more pleasant.

"Hope everything goes well," Willa said in return.

"Thanks." She draped her parka over her arm and walked outside into the twenty-degree weather.

I looked at Willa. "I'm scared."

Willa snickered. "You knocked her up. The least you can do is roll with the mood swings."

"It's just so unlike her to be moody."

"Be patient. I love you."

"Love you too." I gave her one more kiss and slipped into my coat before stepping out the door.

RELEASE THE HONEY BADGER

WILLA

"Travis is stopping by," Oliver informed me as he walked into the kitchen, kissing my shoulder while I stood at the counter, stirring my hot cocoa.

I dropped the spoon and spun to face him. "Wait. What? Why? I didn't know he was in the area."

"He and Addie still hang out pretty regularly."

I frowned. "Doesn't it piss you off that they aren't together? I mean, look at everything they did to you, and for what? A fling?" I was getting heated.

Oliver's hands ran down my shoulders to rest at my elbows. "Down, girl," he teased.

I glared at him, and he relented. "Yes, Willa. It infuriates me sometimes, but I keep coming back to where we are today and how happy I am. Willa, *you* are my future, so what do I care what they did in the past."

"You're too forgiving for your own good."

"And you love me anyway," he said, pressing his lips against mine. I wrapped my arms around his neck, and he picked me up, sitting me on the counter next to my drink.

"How much time do we have before he gets here?"

Bella barked from the living room just before a knock came to the front door.

Oliver frowned. "I'm guessing that's him."

I didn't let go. "Can't we tell him to go away?"

Oliver grinned and pressed another kiss to my lips before pulling out of my grip. "Be nice."

"Didn't my momma warn you? I don't play well with others."

He laughed. "That's not exactly what she said. She said you protect the people you love with the ferocity of a honey badger. Which made me look up honey badgers, and that's a terrifying compliment. I think." He booped me on the nose before rushing off to answer the door.

I slid from the counter to finish stirring my hot cocoa. I heard Oliver answer the door and decided it would probably be rude if I didn't say hi. He *was* Oliver's best friend.

They were standing just inside the door as I walked into the living room. Travis waved to me, and I gave him a half-smile. I didn't analyze many people, but I analyzed the shit out of Travis every time I saw him. I knew Oliver had forgiven him, but I hadn't forgiven him for hurting Oliver.

Oliver was over six feet, and Travis had several inches on him and nearly eighty pounds. Oliver's muscles were tightly compacted, while Travis was bulky. His broad shoulders to waist ratio reminded me of a superhero's physique. It was over the top, and I wondered how much time it took to maintain. All he needed was a grossly caramelized tan, and he'd fit right in at a bodybuilding competition. Okay, maybe he wasn't that veiny, but it wouldn't take much.

By all rights, Travis should look intimidating, but he had sad brown eyes that coerced people into wanting to heal his fractured heart. And the way he grinned made even strangers feel as if they shared a special connection. The smile he gave me now wasn't exactly flirtatious but made me feel seen. I wasn't impervious to him, but I saw him for what he was, and it made me cautious.

He was a little cracked, but not so broken that people avoided him. It was the opposite. People were drawn to his mystery, craving a peek inside his cracked exterior to discover the secrets dangling just out of reach. I could see how someone might trip over themselves trying to be the one to fix him.

While he made everyone else feel seen, he didn't let many people close enough to see him, but he'd let Addison in, and I acknowledged the depth of what that meant. I also grasped the heady temptation he posed for Addison and saw how she could fall for his whole thing.

I didn't trust him. Where Oliver grew up polished, Travis had rough edges he'd learned to hide. But I recognized them because we had that in common. Travis would be one to throw down, where Oliver would try to defuse the fight before it began. Maybe that's why the two of them got along so well. They balanced each other.

Travis had always been polite to me and I to him, but I didn't like him. And I suspected he knew where we stood.

Travis said, "I left it in the car. I wasn't sure what you wanted to do."

Oliver nodded. "I'll come get it."

"Get what?" I asked.

Oliver gave me a sly smile. "Nothing."

My eyebrows rose. "Is it my present?"

"Eh . . ."

Oliver was sexy. He was sweet. He was smart and kind and amazing in bed. Oliver was great at a lot of things, but he was *not* good at keeping secrets. And he was especially bad at keeping surprises a surprise. I learned this about him very quickly.

Travis laughed. "Dude, you suck."

I smiled. "He couldn't bluff to save his life."

Oliver looked between us, his mouth open like he was going to argue, but he snapped it shut and walked out of the house.

I laughed, and before following after him, Travis said, "He tries."

I peeked out the window, trying to get a glimpse of whatever it was, but they angled their bodies, blocking me from seeing anything. If Travis was bringing it to him, it probably had something to do with computers. *Did he buy me a new laptop?* The oven timer went off, and I ran to the kitchen to remove the cookies before they burned. Several minutes later, Oliver came back inside alone and empty-handed.

"What was that?" I asked as he came toward me.

He wrapped his arms around me. "Don't worry about it?"

I pulled back. "You're trying really hard to keep it a secret, and I'm proud of you so I won't pry, but I'm so curious."

He started opening his mouth, and I interrupted, pressing my fingers to his lips. "Don't tell me."

He smiled. "You'll find out soon enough, but I sent it with Travis so I wouldn't be tempted."

I smirked, pushing up on my toes and kissing him. "Proud of you."

CHRISTMAS SPIRIT

Oliver

A BLANKET of white mist hung in the morning air, hiding everything beyond the front yard. I walked down the porch steps with Bella until the cloud enveloped us. I started a slow jog down the sidewalk, worried we'd collide with someone in the dense fog. I had my running vest on. The one Addison had insisted I wear. It was an obnoxious blinking monstrosity, but it was created for mornings like this one. It was too early for traffic, but there were a few cars that passed by, their lights flickering beacons in the fog. It was an eerie run, and Bella didn't seem to like it either.

But if I was spending most of the day in the car, I needed a brief run.

I hadn't let Willa know how nervous I was about our trip. My parents were wonderful people. They divorced when I was a teen but remained friends even after they both remarried. It was unusual, but it worked for them.

We were staying at my dad's house. I'd always been closer to him than my mom. Both of my parents had welcomed Travis and Addison with open arms, and I knew they would love Willa, too.

Most people wouldn't invite their ex—and the best friend she cheated with—home for the holidays, but Addison and Travis had become staples in our lives and were practically family. Travis had been around for nearly twenty-six years and Addison had been there for the last eleven. My parents claimed them as their own. And my sister saw them as her siblings, even though she had never been particularly close to either of them.

Addison's father was angry over our breakup, and it left a palpable tension in their family. Meanwhile, Travis had enough heartbreak in the past year. I was afraid one more loss would break him completely.

They both seemed miserable and repentant, and I couldn't bring myself to turn my sister and parents against them. I didn't want my family to hate them. I was still angry with both of them, but not angry enough to tear them away from the only family they had left.

But, keeping the truth to ourselves painted Willa and me in a bad light. As far as my family was concerned, Addison was having my baby, and I was gallivanting around with another woman. At least that's how I imagined they saw it.

I was hoping when they met Willa, they would see what I saw and understand why we were together. They would even see how Addison supported our relationship, and I was hoping they'd jump on board. It's not like I'd abandoned Addison. She wasn't in love with me. She was only in love with the idea of me, and of course, we cared about each other, but we both deserved more than that.

We deserved to be happy.

I arrived back at the house, and Bella ran to find Willa while I removed my jacket. I pulled my shirt over my head as I followed her, finding both dog and woman in the bathroom. Willa was packing her bathroom essentials.

Stepping into the room, I pressed a kiss to Willa's cheek and stepped toward the shower. "I'm gonna shower really quick."

She bit her lip, watching as I stripped down. She stepped forward. "Do you want me to join you?"

"Of course I do."

She shook her head. "Dammit, I can't. I just did my hair. I have to look my best if I'm going to meet the people who created you. Especially because they already think I'm a homewrecker."

"They know you aren't a homewrecker."

"That's what you say, but I have my doubts. You told me they love Addison, and I know how bad this looks from the outside. It's not going to be like Thanksgiving was at my parent's. Are you sure I should go?"

"I don't want to spend the holidays without you." I took a breath. "If I don't go because I'm here with you, then it'll be the first Christmas I miss, and that's not gonna look good. It's not that I need them to approve, but I want them to love you. And if they think you're the reason I'm not coming home—"

"I get it." she sighed. "I don't like it, but I do get it."

I pulled her closer, and her hands wrapped around to squeeze my ass. "I love you," I whispered against her lips. "I wouldn't invite you to come if I thought they wouldn't love you. All they need is to meet you, and they'll understand."

She narrowed her eyes. "I know what you're doing." In a deep voice, she said, "I know. If I get all naked and sexy, it'll make Willa forget how bad of an idea this is."

I leaned in, grinning against her lips as I kissed her. "Is it working?"

"Ha!" She pushed away from me. "Take a shower. We'll talk once you have clothes on."

"Or, you could take yours off."

"Shut up and get in the shower. I need to go feed Bella."

She left the room before I could say any more, and I stepped into the shower.

WE DROPPED Bella at Willa's parent's house before heading for Upstate New York. We took Willa's new car because the gas mileage was better than my truck. It was almost a seven-hour drive, and the holiday traffic wasn't too terrible.

About an hour into the trip, Willa switched the music. "I can't handle anymore damn Christmas songs."

"But, it's getting us in the Christmas spirit!"

"My Christmas spirit is just fine," she grumbled.

"You just started listening to it way too soon, so you're sick of it."

"You might be right, but right now, it's putting me in a bad mood."

"Why?"

Willa shook her head. "I don't know. My stomach kinda hurts and I'm really nervous about meeting your family."

"You're stressing over nothing. They're going to love you."

"And if they don't?"

"What's the worst that could happen?"

"Being with me could alienate you from your family and force you to choose between us."

I shook my head. "I shouldn't ask you those kinds of questions. Of course you'd come up with something like that." I'd had a similar thought, but I knew it would never come to that. My family was more accepting than most. I squeezed her thigh. "Willa, it'll be fine. I promise. My parents are divorced and remarried, and the four of them get along just fine. If they can make that work, we can do this."

"Just don't abandon me with them, please."

"I'll be by your side every step of the way."

She looked at me. "Promise?"

"I promise."

SHE LOVES TO BAKE. I LOVE TO EAT.

WILLA

WE ARRIVED at Oliver's dad's in the early evening. The ranch-style home wasn't huge, but looked like a typical middle-class American home. I think I was expecting something more intimidating, not that it wasn't nice. A three-car garage opened off the side of the house, leaving lots of extra room for additional parking in the driveway. Oliver wrapped his arm around my shoulder as he led me to the door. Just outside, I said, "I've never been so nervous about meeting someone's parents."

"Shh," he kissed me. "They'll love you."

With a flash of a smile, Oliver turned and reached for the door. Before he touched the knob, the door swung open. A burly man filled the opening. He was tall and handsome like Oliver, but he carried an extra eighty pounds, and his dark hair was dusted with silver.

"Hey, dad," Oliver said, squeezing my shoulder. "This is Willa."

His dad pulled us in out of the cold and hugged Oliver. His wife, Janet, gave me a warm smile. She had short brown hair and stylish hot-pink framed glasses. "Hi Willa, I'm Janet. Oliver's stepmom, though he was basically grown by the time I came into the picture. Anyway, it's nice to finally meet you. I'm a hugger. Can I hug you?"

"Of course."

It was an awkward hug, but I was relieved to feel accepted. Oliver's dad was next, wrapping me up in a quick bearhug before stepping back. "I'm Buck." He looked up at Oli, saying, "Where's all your stuff?"

"It's still in the car. I thought we'd get settled in, and I'd bring it in later."

Buck said, "We aren't gonna bite her. You can go get it now."

Oliver looked unsure.

I shrugged. "I can help you."

"Nonsense." Buck slipped into his coat. "I'll help him while you ladies chat."

Oliver glanced at me. I gave him a reassuring nod, and he followed his dad.

Once they were gone, Janet said, "I can take your coat."

I slipped out of it and handed it to her. She placed it in a closet and led me into the kitchen.

"Oh, it smells so good in here," I noted.

"I've been baking all day. Help yourself." She waved her arm toward the counter where an assortment of cookies lay on platters and in tins. "I always make more than we could possibly eat."

I smiled, picking up a tree-shaped sugar cookie covered in fluffy green icing and topped with sprinkles. "My mom and I bake cookies together every year. She loves to bake, and I love to eat, though, we give most of them away."

Janet laughed. "Match made in heaven." She sighed. "I wish my girls were around to help me bake, but they both live out on the West coast and don't like to travel here until it's above seventy degrees."

"That must be hard to be so far away."

She shrugged. "It is what it is. I still FaceTime with them at least once a week., but they've grown closer to their father since they've been adults. We've been divorced for nearly fifteen years, but he's still single, and I don't think the girls ever got over me falling in love with someone else. Don't get me wrong, they like Buck, but I think they feel a certain loyalty to their father. He always was a better father than he was a husband."

I frowned, unsure how it would feel to watch your parents split up and then see one of them move on while the other wallowed. I guess I would gravitate toward the heart-broken parent, too. "How long have you and Buck been together?"

"We celebrated our eleventh anniversary this past fall."

"Oh, wow, so you've known Oliver for quite some time."

"Oh, yes."

That meant she also knew Addison quite well. I fiddled with the cookie in my hand before realizing I hadn't tried it yet. I took a bite and moaned. "Mmm, this is delicious," I said around a full mouth.

"Thank you. It's my granny's old recipe."

"Granny gets five stars." I smiled. Janet was easy to talk to. "Your glasses are cute."

"Oh, thank you. I like bright colors."

"Well, they work for you."

Oliver and Buck walked in with our bags and unloaded them in the bedroom before coming back to join us.

We went out to dinner together, and it was a lovely time. I liked Janet, and if tonight was anything to go by, I had nothing to worry about. Oliver's family was kind, and the trip I had been dreading turned into another exciting first with Oliver. I was excited to spend Christmas with Oliver and his family after all.

WHAT'S MY NAME?

OLIVER

It was a relaxing evening, but as we settled in for the night, I felt weird being back in my childhood bedroom. Almost every time I had stayed here in my adult life, I'd had Addison here with me, and I half expected her to appear out of thin air.

But it was Willa in my bed, and I was both incredibly grateful and terrified I'd call her by the wrong name just out of reflex. That'd be unforgivable, and I knew she wasn't Addison. I was glad she wasn't Addison.

Willa sat in bed, scrolling through her phone, while I pulled my pajamas out of my suitcase.

Before I could change, she looked up at me, her brows folding together. "What's wrong?"

I took a deep breath, hesitating whether it was appropriate to tell her the truth.

"Spit it out," she said. "I can take it."

I watched her, looking so beautiful in the golden lamp-light with her smooth caramel skin and thick wavy hair. Her lashes were long and dark, surrounding even darker eyes. They were bottomless, and if I looked too long, I got lost in their depths. "I'm thrilled you're here."

Those bottomless pits narrowed. "But?"

I let out a breath. "I have a lot of memories here with . . . Addison." I quickly added, "I'm happy it's you here with me now, but . . ."

"Just say it."

"I'm worried I'll slip and call you Addison, and it isn't because I don't love you or am confused about who I'm with. It's just reflex."

She laid her palms on the mattress, running them over its surface. "Even here in this bed?"

I winced, nodding, hating to admit it, but I didn't want to lie. We'd promised each other our ugly truths, and that's what I was giving her.

She grinned, which I wasn't expecting. Then she got on her knees and crawled down the bed toward me. When she got to the end, she leaned back on her knees and stripped out of her shirt, leaving her chest bare. Her grin grew while I held my breath in confusion.

"I guess we'll have to make our own memories, won't we?" She swung her legs off the bed and stood, slinking toward me.

I met her in the middle, already hard for her. I lifted her by the back of her thighs, and her arms went around my shoulders. Our lips met in an urgent kiss. Her nails scraped up my scalp as I carried her back to bed. She pulled back abruptly. "What's my name?" she purred.

"Willa," I panted.

She gave me a seductive smile and yanked at my shirt, pulling it up. I laid her back on the bed, and she arched her spine, showing off the curves of her body. She ran her hands down her abdomen to hook into the top of her night shorts. I groaned and whipped my shirt over my head before helping her out of her shorts.

I pulled away to admire the view and also to remove my pants. She followed me up, her eyes intent on me unfastening my jeans. As soon as I pushed my jeans and boxers down, she leaned forward, wrapping a firm hand around my shaft.

Those seductress eyes looked up at me. "What's my name, Oliver?"

"Fuuuck Willa."

She grinned and leaned forward, taking me in her mouth.

"God, Willa. You—" I moaned, unable to focus on what I was saying as the hot moisture of her mouth surrounded and tugged at my dick. "Fuuck."

"Mmmm." The vibration of her moan almost sent me over the edge which would've been embarrassing.

"Willa," I warned, and her hands gripped my ass as she took me to the back of her throat. Ironically, I was the one to choke, trying desperately to stop myself from my imminent orgasm.

As if noticing this, she pulled away. Wiping the moisture from her mouth, she demanded, "Lie down!"

While she crawled up the bed, I went around the side and slid onto the mattress, lying back. My hands went to her waist as she mounted me. She gripped my shaft in her hand

and directed it to her entrance, but paused. "What's my name?"

"Willa."

She removed her hand and lowered her hips, only taking in the tip. I looked up at her, and she raised a brow.

"Willa," I panted.

She grinned and sunk all the way down. I groaned her name again. She wasn't a dominatrix, but I would've done anything to keep her moving. Her name was a constant whisper on my lips, and as my release finally came, it was to her name.

UNGODLY AMOUNTS OF SUGAR

WILLA

THE SUN WAS SHINING through the window, and I looked at the clock. It was already ten. We'd overslept. I turned over to wake Oliver and found his spot empty.

I reached for my phone, seeing he'd sent me a text an hour ago. It said he went to go pick up firewood with his dad and he'd be back soon. I figured he must be back by now. I jumped out of bed and threw a sweatshirt over my tank top and pajama bottoms. I went in search of Oliver. I heard female voices on my way to the kitchen, and sure enough, two women I hadn't met were standing at the oversized island.

Their backs were to me, and I was about to say hello when the one about my age said, "You'd think she'd try to make a good impression meeting his family for the first time, but then again, what can you really expect from a home-wrecker?"

I stifled my hello and backtracked, retreating into the dining room where I was hidden. My mind was spinning. They had to be talking about me. Who else could it be? But I hoped that they were talking about someone else.

"Addison spoiled us. No one will beat her. I don't know what that son of mine is thinking."

I covered my mouth with both hands.

"It should be interesting seeing how she and Oli react when Addison gets here."

I backed toward the hall before spinning around and rushing back to the bedroom. It was just what I'd feared. His family wasn't happy about me being here, and this was going to be an excruciating holiday.

I sent a text to Oliver as soon as I got to the bedroom, asking when he'd be back. After several minutes of no response, I decided I was too furious to call him right now. He said he wouldn't leave my side. But he had.

I took a shower while I awaited a response, but there was still no answer even after I got out of the shower. I got ready for the day, worrying over which outfit would be just right to meet the family who didn't want to meet me. Was there a suitable outfit for that? I doubted it.

Deep breaths, I reminded myself. I ended up putting on my favorite outfit. It was the most flattering. I was saving it for Christmas day, but I had to do something to impress these people.

After the year I'd had, and everything I'd learned about being comfortable in my own skin, here I was trying to dazzle these bitchy women. I'd made a promise I wouldn't compromise my self-worth to make others happy, but Oliver was important to me. I understood why these women were protective of him, but they also had unfairly pegged me as the enemy.

My phone chimed.

On our way back.

That told me nothing. On their way back could mean five minutes to an hour.

I typed back. *How long?*

Fifteen minutes

I did my makeup and dried my hair in loose waves. And after fifteen minutes, I left the bedroom. I figured I could stand a few minutes with Oliver's sister and mom before he got here, and I didn't want it to look like I was hiding.

I found the women in the living room. They all turned to stare at me as I walked into the room. Janet was there, and another man I didn't know but figured was Harry, Oliver's stepdad. "Hi," I offered with a little wave.

"Good morning, Willa," Janet called. "There are leftovers from breakfast in the kitchen. I can warm something up for you." She started getting up.

I waved her away. "Oh, no. That's okay. I'm not hungry. Thank you." Once she sat down, I continued, "Sorry, I slept so late. I never sleep in. I guess I was catching up on sleep."

Harry—I thought—was reading the newspaper grandpa style and flipped the page, shaking it in a firm motion to straighten it. "Actually," he said, without looking away from his reading. "That's a myth. You can't catch up on sleep. There was a recent study that getting extra sleep to overcome sleep deprivation doesn't work."

"Oh," I smiled, uncomfortable. Nobody else said anything, so I asked, "You must be Kim, Shelby, and Harry?"

"That's us," Kim chimed from her place on the couch.

She didn't look old enough to be Oliver's mom. She wore her short blonde hair in a stylish bob, and though her outfit was casual, her clothes were expensive. Even lounging, she looked polished and professional. The way she held herself and her classic beauty brought to mind an old-time film actress from Hollywood's Golden Age. And from where I stood, I couldn't spot a wrinkle on her unblemished face.

Oliver had inherited many of her features, though none were as significant as the stunning blue eyes. It was as if Oliver's eyes shown from his mother's face, and I realized, other than his coloring and his height, he mirrored his mother in a much more masculine way.

"Nice to meet you, Willow," Shelby added.

I looked at his sister. "It's actually Willa."

She shrugged. "Willa, Willow, close enough."

Shelby was a few years older than Oliver and me. She was beautiful like her mother, and I saw both Kim and Buck in her features, but the bitchiness was all her own. She wore her long auburn curls loose around her shoulders, and though she gave me a fleeting smile, soon her lips melted back into a perma-scowl, which seemed much more natural on her.

Out of nowhere, a girl about five years old with shoulder-length brown curls and a face covered with chocolate came screaming into the room and slammed into me, shouting, "Surprise hug!" She wrapped her arms around me in a bear hug, pressing her face right into the front of my cream-colored sweater.

I sucked in a breath, and before I could hug the girl back, she pushed off me, running back the way she came.

Everyone laughed, except for me. I was trying to assess the damage to my shirt.

Shelby laughed. "That girl is so affectionate. Even to strangers."

Janet asked, "Was that the chocolate pudding I asked her not to get into?"

I looked down at the chocolate pudding smeared across the front of my sweater and let out a breath, trying to calm myself. This wasn't going as I'd planned. *And where was Oliver?* I wanted to go back—to rewind to Thanksgiving, or even to five minutes ago so I could stay hidden in the bedroom.

"Don't mind her. That's just our Cadence. We call her Cady," Kim said about Shelby's daughter.

"She's already hopped up on sugar, and we haven't even started the gingerbread houses," Janet said with a sigh.

Shelby added, "Her dad's supposed to be picking her up in a couple of hours, and I like to send her with him juiced up on energy so he sees what I'm dealing with on a daily basis."

I took a few steps back so I could see into the dining room where Cadence was coloring at the table. There was a dog I'd never seen before chewing on crayons under Cady's chair. As if sensing my attention, the dog jumped up and ran to me. It was white and fuzzy, some kind of designer poodle mix that I couldn't name.

As soon as the dog got to me, it jumped up, and I scratched its head. The little girl turned around and said, "That's Fluffy. He's my dog. My daddy got him for me."

I stood between the two rooms listening to both Cady

and the adults in the living room who were bashing Cady's father as if his daughter wasn't within hearing range.

I tried to distract the little girl by asking questions. "What kind of dog is Fluffy?"

The dog was still jumping on me, and I tried as politely as possible to get him to stop, but kneeling only had him in my face and snagging my sweater. Standing up had him jumping, and I didn't even hear Cady's answer.

"How old is he?" I asked.

I tried to keep the dog at a distance by holding onto his collar, but he was too wiggly, and I only hurt my wrist. Then I tried to ignore the dog altogether, but that prompted him to latch onto my leg.

Cady was guessing about his age. "He's younger than me because I got him for my birthday, but my daddy said I have to keep him at mommy's a'cause his girlfriend is lalergic."

The damn dog began humping my leg. I tried to pull away, not caring if I looked rough. The dog was molesting me in a room full of people, and no one was paying any attention except Cady, who was unfazed by the dog's behavior, announcing, "I think I can get Daddy to buy a friend for Fluffy. I just have to tell him how much I want one and how much Mommy says she hates Fluffy."

My god, these people were awful. I loved dogs and kids but didn't necessarily like either of these.

Roaring laugher caught my attention from the other room, and I thought maybe they caught on to the fact that the dog was molesting me, but nope. Harry was doing an impression of the dog-buying ex-husband.

Dear Jesus, how did Oliver turn out okay?

I finally limped into the dining room, towing the dog

along. I pealed the horny bastard off my leg, scolding it in a firm voice, "No! Bad dog!"

It worked at least temporarily, and the dog backed off until Cady giggled and jumped out of her chair, running up next to me to yell, "No, bad dog! Bad, bad dog!" She waved her hand at him, but in her high-pitched voice, the dog thought she was playing and ran at her. Cady squealed and ran for the living room. The dog chased after her, and I stepped back into the living room in time to watch Cady jump up on Kim's lap, squealing with laughter as the dog jumped on top of both of them. Kim shoved the dog to the floor, and Fluffy grabbed a stray throw pillow and ran into the dining room with it. I moved to get it before the dog had a chance to tear it up, but Fluffy had already mounted the pillow and was humping vigorously. I retreated, trying my best to smile as Kim started tickling her granddaughter.

"What happened to your pants?" Shelby asked me.

I looked down only to realize that fucking dog had ripped a hole in my favorite pair of leggings. I shook my head. "Fluffy jumped on me."

Shelby gave an exaggerated nod. "Oh, yeah. You have to watch for him."

I have to watch for him. What about keeping an eye on your own damn dog? I was so close to saying it aloud. My entire outfit was ruined, and yet everyone else looked put together.

This was a disaster. It made me miss the loveless holidays with Evan and his family. They may have been ambivalent, but at least they were polite to my face. These people had it out for me, or maybe it was just the universe telling me to run.

Where the fuck was Oliver?

I pulled out my phone and sent him another text. Almost immediately, my phone rang. "Hello."

"Willa, I'm so sorry." Oliver sounded out of breath. "We got caught up. We're on our way back. I'll be there in five minutes. Have my sister and mom arrived yet?"

"Yes, they've been here for a while."

"Shit," he said. "I'll be there soon."

"Okay."

When I hung up, all eyes were on me. "They're on their way back," I said, in case they were wondering.

Janet gave a friendly smile while Kim asked, "Has anyone heard when Addison is due to arrive?"

Shelby said, "She told me Travis was making the trip with her. It's no wonder she doesn't want to make that long of a drive by herself, especially while she's this far along. I mean, she could go into labor at any moment. I'm surprised Oliver didn't offer to bring her."

I couldn't hold my tongue on that one. "She still has six weeks before she's due. Oliver went with her to her checkup last Thursday and everything looked great, so I don't think either of them were worried about her making the trip alone. But Oliver did offer. Addison refused. She already planned on making the trip with Travis."

Shelby frowned. "Addison wanted to make sure Travis didn't spend the holidays alone. That's sweet."

"Awe," Kim sighed, "She's so kind to look after her friend that way. Poor guy has been through enough in the last year."

Shelby added, "Oliver really dropped the ball on that one."

I swallowed, biting my tongue.

"Uncle Oli dropped what ball?" Cady asked.

"Oh, Cadence, men are idiots. Remember that." Shelby stood from the couch. "Let's do mimosas."

As everyone stood, I walked back toward the bedroom, but Janet stopped me. "Don't worry about your clothes. Mimosas help with all life's little problems." Janet looped her arm through mine, insisting, "Come on, Willa. It's a family tradition to have mimosas on Christmas Eve's eve." Her smile was so friendly that I thought maybe I was judging everyone too fast.

I nodded. "Mimosas, it is."

As soon as we walked into the kitchen, Shelby announced, "I got sparkling grape juice for Addison so she won't feel left out." She looked at me as she said it, so there was no misconstruing her meaning. They accommodated Addie because she was one of them, and they planned to keep her around. Preferably without me.

Kim gave Cadence a piggyback ride into the kitchen and immediately let the horny dog outside. I was relieved.

"So, Willa, does your family have any holiday traditions other than cookie baking?" Janet asked.

Kim said, "Like drinking mimosas?"

"Not mimosas, but my mom makes fresh apple cider every year, and now we spike it with rum."

"Mmm, spiked hot apple cider sounds delicious."

Shelby poured the drinks, saying, "No thanks. I'll stick to mimosas."

She passed them out and held hers up. "To having the entire family together for the holidays." She glanced at me, "And Willa, of course."

"Cheers," Kim repeated.

As soon as we took our drinks, cars pulled into the driveway. Finally, Oliver was back.

The garage door opened and a moment later, Buck walked into the kitchen from the garage. Right behind him was Oliver, Addison, and Travis.

Great. This day couldn't get any better. Everyone swarmed the three of them, giving hugs and exchanging hellos.

"Addison, it's so nice to see you," his sister gushed, rushing to hug Addison. When she pulled back, Kim came in for a hug with Cady still on her back.

"Auntie Addie, you got a big belly."

Everyone laughed at that, and Shelby laid her hand on Addison's belly. "Ohh, you make the most beautiful pregnant woman. Why couldn't I have looked that cute when I was pregnant?"

"Oh, hush," Addison said. "You were gorgeous when pregnant, and I can only dream of bouncing back as quickly as you did."

"Willa, do you want kids?" Kim asked, and all eyes turned to me.

I swallowed, glancing at Oliver, who seemed like he was still miles away. He winced while I choked down another tough pill before addressing the question. "Someday."

"Well, better be sooner than later, or all your lady parts will shrivel up," Shelby said. "And you'd better start preparing because Oliver's going to be a dad in a few short months. If you're not ready for kids, then jump ship now."

I looked at Addison, and even she looked uncomfortable. I gave her a small smile, trying to be as genuine as possible. "I can't wait to meet baby Emerson."

Addison's smile faltered as Oliver finally made his way to me and wrapped his arm around my shoulder, kissing the side of my head. I watched as the whole room took in Addison's reaction, and then the eyes were back on me, unfriendly stares of apprehension. These people were loyal to their own but made it clear I wasn't one of them.

I felt like I was back in middle school, and the popular girls were telling me I wasn't good enough to hang with them. Only now, no one was actually saying those words to my face, so maybe those middle school girls were better. At least I knew where I stood.

Oliver seemed oblivious to the attention as he appraised me. "What happened to you?"

I took a deep breath, looking down at my ruined outfit. "Oh, yeah. I need to go change." I set down the mimosa I'd barely sipped and escaped, dragging Oliver with me.

"Are you okay?" he asked once we got to the bedroom.

I closed the door and spun on him. "No, I'm not okay! I've been molested by a dog. A hellion child ruined my favorite shirt, and your sister has been a real treat. I spent all of fifteen minutes with those people, and I wish I would've stuck to my guns and stayed home. They're awful, Oliver. I don't know how you turned out okay. And why the hell did you leave me? You promised!"

He swallowed. "I'm sorry, Willa. I wanted you to relax and sleep in. I thought our trip would only be a half-hour, and I'd be back before you woke, but we ran into some old friends, and everything took longer. I tried to call, but the cell reception was shoddy." He shook his head, heavy with regret. He stepped forward, pulling me in. "I'm so sorry, Willa. I won't leave you again."

I didn't believe him. "They're diabolical, Oliver. I guarantee you, your sister has a plan to get you and Addie back together."

"It's not gonna happen, and you, me, and Addie know that. My family will figure it out too. Give them a little grace to adjust."

"That's easy for you to say. They love you. I'm some homewrecker that broke up your marriage."

His eyes narrowed. "Did they say that?"

I nodded. "They didn't know I was listening." I shrugged. "Or maybe they did. I don't know." I threw my arms out in exasperation.

Oliver straightened, his fist clenching. He started walking for the door.

I grabbed his wrist. "What are you doing?"

"I'm gonna give them a piece of my mind."

I tugged him toward me. "Please don't. You're just going to paint an even bigger target on my back. They already hate me."

"I'm sure they don't hate you, but I won't let them talk shit about you."

"Great, then stick by my side and protect me, but don't go out there guns blazing, or they'll just say I pussy whipped you or something."

I opened the closet and began searching through my suitcase for something else to wear. "Do you know what the plans are today?"

"My mom and Harry are leaving in a bit to spend the afternoon with Harry's kids. The rest of us are making gingerbread houses until Cadence's dad gets here to pick her up. He's not very reliable. If we have time, we're going ice skating, and then we'll come back here for dinner before heading to the Christmas light show where Mom, Harry, and his family will meet up with us."

"Are Addison's parents coming, too?"

He scoffed, shaking his head. "No, they have much fancier holiday plans, and her dad isn't pleased about how things turned out between Addie and me."

"Well, I'm relieved they won't be there. What about Fluffy? Is he staying all day?"

"Yes, but he usually wears himself out around now and sleeps all afternoon. And I'll protect you from him. Is Cady the one who ruined your sweater?"

I nodded. "It's cashmere. I splurged on it, and I'm worried it's ruined."

"Do we need to go out shopping?"

"No, it's fine. I packed ten days' worth of clothes, but I just wanted to impress everyone. I guess I was hoping they were all as nice as Janet."

"Give them time," he encouraged.

I stared at him, chewing on my lip. We were fighting a battle with our arms tied behind our backs. "Oliver, without them knowing that Addie cheated, we look like the bad guys. I'm the homewrecker or the rebound, but either way, they don't think I'll stick around."

"Then we'll have to prove them wrong." He kissed me. "Get changed and let's go build a gingerbread house."

I sighed. "That could be fun."

I got dressed, and we joined the others in the foyer where Kim and Harry were saying their goodbyes. Kim hugged Oliver but didn't spare me a glance before walking out the door. Everyone who remained gravitated toward the kitchen, where Janet was setting out all the makings of a gingerbread village.

"Cadence, baby, come sit over here. I have everything set up for you," Janet called.

"Thanks, Grandma."

Janet had already baked the gingerbread pieces, so the rest of us just needed to put them together. While Janet and Buck helped Cadence at the oversized kitchen island, Oliver and I made our own house at one end of the kitchen table. Meanwhile, Shelby roped Addison into making one with her at the other end.

Travis was the last to enter the kitchen, and he took it in with a groan, "Buck, they got you too?"

Buck shrugged, spackling icing on the edges of the gingerbread. "Grandchildren. What can I say?"

While Addison was already hard at work, Shelby sat back, taking a sip of her drink. "You can help us?" she offered.

Travis glanced at them. Addison was too focused on the challenge in front of her and didn't appear to be listening. "Addison's in the zone. I doubt she'll even let *you* help, Shel."

"That's the goal," she said, making herself comfortable in her chair.

Travis pulled up a stool on the other side of the island. "I'm not gonna be left out. I'll make my own gingerbread thing."

Oliver and I worked well together. We usually did, and our house came together much faster than I'd expected. I didn't want to be that overly affectionate couple who annoyed everyone else, but it was hard not to flirt a little.

I was placing gumdrops on the roof when Oliver said, "Open up."

He had a hand full of red hots, which he knew were my favorite. I opened my mouth, and he tossed one up. I leaned forward and caught it.

"Score," Oliver said.

As I chewed, I said, "Your turn."

I tossed a gumdrop at him, and it bounced off his lip. "Gotta be quicker than that."

"That toss was terrible!" he complained.

"Here, we'll find out who's better," I said as I added a licorice basketball hoop to our house, and then we scooted back from the table and took turns throwing the red hots. Oliver had much better aim, and I ended up knocking the hoop down with my badly thrown red hots.

Cadence had already eaten an ungodly amount of sugar and, after about an hour, lost interest in the Gingerbread house altogether, deciding to tear out part of the wall so she could eat it.

She came to look at our gingerbread house, and before she could destroy it, she spotted my phone. "Do you have games on your phone?"

"I sure do." Thanks to Jodi's kids, I'd downloaded several kid's games. And after Jodi's oldest spent seventy-eight dollars on a game called *Princess Gumdrop Rainbow Sparkle,* I'd learned how to password protect it to prevent kids from buying things like banana truffle points.

So when Cady asked, "Can I play a game?"

I opened up the game folder and handed it to her. She played for a little while, but the sugar kept her from staying in one spot for too long. She was all over the kitchen and eventually got bored, abandoning my phone on the counter across the room. She cranked up the background music when "Frosty the Snowman" came on, dancing and spinning while she sang the wrong lyrics at the top of her lungs.

Shelby grabbed Cady's coat and sent her outside to run around the yard with the dog, which must've sounded fun in her sugar high because she took off out the door. I was worried she'd puke, but as soon as the door closed, Shelby said, "That bastard better be here soon. I didn't get her all hopped up on sugar, so I'd have to deal with her."

If she wasn't already drunk, she was close. Addison was still hard at work. Shelby grabbed for candy on the island and gasped. "Dear God! What is that monstrosity?"

She was looking at Travis's gingerbread creation. Buck blocked my view, so I leaned to the side to get a look.

"It's a fort for the Gingerbread soldiers," Travis answered.

Unlike most gingerbread houses which were colorful and bright, his was mostly blacks and browns with a hint of red. It was a two-story structure with a flat roof and dark candy cane bars covering the windows. Travis had gingerbread men standing guard on top of the fort with candy guns. Spiked candy canes surrounded them, and black licorice spun around the top to look like barbed wire. He had a flag made of red fruit leather and decorated with black icing.

"It looks like a prison," Shelby noted.

Travis shook his head. "It's not, but they do have cells. These gingerbread men on top are carrying the highest grade candy cane Uzis, and they're pretty trigger happy. So I doubt there will be any survivors to lock up."

Shelby gawked at him. "You took this to a dark place, T."

"Well, I think it's very creative, Travis," Janet praised.

Travis grinned. "I was just thinking outside the box."

"What's the flag supposed to say?" Addison asked from her spot at the table.

"It's a no eating sign."

Addison laughed. "Is that what it is?"

Travis huffed, "It's hard to get the icing not to smear on that fruit stuff."

Oliver laughed, and I couldn't help but smile.

Travis stood, moving toward Addison. "And what does your house look like? All pristine and perfect?"

Addie smiled. "Yes, with a whimsical twist."

If this were a competition, Addison would win. While our simple one-story house was cute, Addison had built a three-level home, each level whimsically smaller than the one before. The amount of iced detail she captured in such a short time was incredible. It was bright and fun, looking like a Christmas decoration one would find at a store.

It put ours to shame.

Travis looked closely at Addison's masterpiece like he was trying to pick it apart, finally settling on, "It's too perfect. Nothing is that perfect."

While the rest of them started discussing the level of detail, I leaned into Oliver. "Oh, wow," I whispered. "That blows ours out of the water."

He shook his head. "I like ours better," he said back. "You know, this is the first year I've gotten to participate. I always partnered with Addison, and she's a perfectionist with a vision. I was her gopher, but this . . . ." He pointed to our simple house. "This we made as a team, and we had fun doing it. I don't care if our house isn't perfect. I love that we built it together."

Oh, my heart.

Buck stood from his spot and stretched. "This is all the gingerbread making I can handle for the day. Shelby, have you heard from Brad yet?"

She was looking at her phone when she answered, "He just texted. He's on his way to get her now."

"She just threw up in the backyard," Addison said, peeking out the window with Travis.

Shelby rolled her eyes. "Of course, she did."

Travis' lip curled, and he added, "Fluffy is eating it."

Shelby groaned. "Damn dog!" She went out into the backyard, and no one else moved.

"Should we go help her?" I asked.

Buck rolled his neck. "Go for it. I don't do puke, and it's Shelby's fault for letting her get all sugared up."

Shelby came back in with a crying Cadence, towing her back toward the bedrooms.

CADENCE'S DAD finally showed up, and she had to take a puke bucket with her in the car because of Shelby's excellent parenting style.

We ate a light lunch of salads and sandwiches. It was way healthier than the things my parents made around the holidays, but it was all excellent. We sat around the table which had been wiped clean from our gingerbread messes.

"Those glasses are cute too," I said, wondering, "How many pairs do you have?"

Janet fingered her glasses. The ones she had on were purple plaid to match her purple shirt. She laughed. "Oh, hun, these are just readers. I have old eyes and am blind as a bat when it comes to reading. I have probably twenty pairs."

"Yeah, a pair for each outfit," Buck said.

She nodded. "That's probably true."

In an abrupt topic change, Shelby said, "We aren't all going to fit in one car?"

Oliver said, "We're driving separate. We have a few things we need to pick up from the store."

"Okay, so that leaves Dad, Janet, me, Addison—"

"Um," Addison interrupted, "I think I'm going to sit this one out."

"What?" Shelby gasped, "No. Come on. You never miss this."

"Yeah, but I'm kinda tired, and I don't even know if my swollen feet will fit into ice skates."

"Addison, you're going," Shelby said, not taking no for an answer. "Travis, are you going?"

"Hell no! You know balancing on tiny blades isn't my strong suit."

Addison jumped at the opportunity. "See, I'll stay and keep Travis company."

Travis clarified, "I'm actually leaving. I'm just not going ice skating."

I didn't miss Addison's look of surprise. "Where are you going?"

"Meeting up with someone?"

"Ooh," Shelby singsonged, "Who's the lucky lady?"

"None of your business," he sang right back.

Giving up on him, Shelby narrowed her efforts on Addison. "You love skating."

"You should come," I encouraged.

She looked at me, giving me a long look before nodding. "Okay."

"Perfect," Shelby concluded before finding her next victim. "So, Travis, who is it that you're meeting up with?"

"An old friend. I figured I'd catch up with her while I was in town."

"Have fun *catching* up." Shelby giggled.

EXPLOSIVE!

Oliver

We left the house in three cars. Willa and I drove separate from the others so we could stop at the store, though it was really more of an excuse to be alone. My dad drove Janet and Shelby, while Addison drove her own car so she could drop Travis off on his date. Their relationship confused me. But I would not let it piss me off. Not tonight.

"Where are Travis and Addison staying?" Willa asked as if reading my mind.

"I'm guessing at her parent's house. I invited Travis to stay with us, but he said he had a place. Maybe he's staying with the girl he's meeting."

"Didn't you ask?"

"No." I glanced at her. "It's not a big deal. If he needed a place, he would've taken my offer."

She sighed. "I guess I'm just curious. So, since we aren't going to the store, where are we going?"

"Oh, we're going to the store. I have to make up for your sweater and leggings."

"That'll take longer than popping in really quick."

I shook my head. "We picked out entire outfits at the thrift store in less than fifteen minutes. I think we can find one simple outfit for you in that amount of time."

She grinned. "In that case, should we get you something too?"

I shrugged, pulling into the strip mall. "If we have time."

The parking lot was packed, and I doubted there would be anything quick about it.

On the way in, she said, "Five bucks on 'Santa Baby.'"

I pursed my lips as I tried to predict what song would come on while we were inside. It's a little competition we'd started. "I'll double that for 'All I Want For Christmas.'"

She groaned. "I think you're gonna win."

"Of course, I will."

As soon as we walked in and I saw the line, I said, "Change of plans. One of us stands in line while the other shops."

"Maybe it's a fast-moving line," she said.

I doubted it. Everyone in line looked way too bored.

I stepped forward and asked the second person in line, "How long have you been waiting?"

"Almost twenty minutes."

"Okay. Thank you." I turned back to Willa. "See, perfect. You get in line and I'll find something for you."

"And why do you get to do the shopping?"

"Because I'm faster."

She looked doubtful. "You don't know what'll fit me."

I snorted. "I pay attention. I know things."

She shook her head as she walked toward the end of the line. "Better not leave me hanging."

And I was off to the women's section. There were so many racks to look through and so little time.

"Hey there, can I help you?" a woman asked. When I looked up, I realized she didn't have a name tag on.

"Do you work here?"

She shook her head. "You just looked a bit frantic. Thought I'd see if I could help."

"I'm shopping for an outfit for my fiancée." In my experience, if a woman was hitting on me—which I wasn't sure if this woman was—they were much less interested if I had a fiancee. Girlfriends didn't have the same effect because girlfriends came and went, but fiancée didn't. So I always had a fiancée.

"Oh, well, she's a lucky lady. I'm surprised she sent you shopping for her." Her hand stroked my arm as she said this.

I was in a hurry and didn't have time to fend her off politely, so I said, "It's my fault. I had a diarrhea explosion and it got everywhere."

Her hand went to her chest as her eyes grew round. She took a quick step back. "What?"

I glanced down at myself. "I probably still have some on me."

She took several steps away. "That's really gross. You shouldn't be in here."

"I gotta make it right for my fiancée."

I wish I could've captured the look on her face before she turned and hurried away. I shook my head. I could've just told her I wasn't interested, but my way was much more effective, and no one's feelings were hurt.

I started flipping through racks when the first cords of "All I Want For Christmas" came on. "Ha! Yes!"

When I glance up, I was getting looks. I needed to tone down the crazy. I found a red sweater tunic thing, and I was sorting through leggings when "Santa Baby" came on over the loudspeaker. "Damn it."

I found her leggings and rushed to the front. I weaved my way to her, and as I approached, I saw the woman from earlier. She jumped out of my way and I smirked. I met up with Willa, who was now third in line.

"Do you hear what's playing right now?" she said with a cocky smirk.

"Yeah, but my song came first."

She laughed. "I guess we tie."

We stepped forward as the line moved, and Willa was looking behind me. "Why is there a woman glaring at us?"

"Oh, I told her I had explosive diarrhea and it got all over both of us."

"What!?"

"She was wasting my time, and I just ran with the first thing that came to mind."

"Which was explosive diarrhea?"

I shrugged. "I guess."

A smile played at her lips like she was suppressing laughter. "Must suck to have beautiful women throw themselves at you everywhere you go."

"Why do you think I'm always having diarrhea?"

She laughed so hard tears leaked from the corners of her eyes.

When we arrived, Janet and Shelby were already skating. My dad had procrastinated putting on his skates, saying he was waiting for everyone to get there.

Willa said, "'You're A Mean One, Mr. Grinch.'"

I thought a moment. "'Let it snow.'"

"Oh good! I'm not too late," Addison said, walking in right behind us, her personal ice skates in hand.

"Those are nice skates," Willa said.

"Thanks. My father has a cabin in Canada. There's a pond that freezes over every winter, so we all have ice skates. Oliver, you didn't bring yours?"

"No, I left them at home. I didn't think about ice skating. The rentals are fine, though."

Willa laughed. "I'm sure yours are better."

I shrugged.

Willa and I sat down on a bench across from Addison. We had our skates almost all the way laced up before I noticed Addison was just sitting there. I looked at her in question.

"I'm going to sit this one out," she said. That's when I realized her belly was preventing her from getting her skates on, and she was too proud to ask for help.

Stubborn Addie never admitted when she needed help. "Here, let me help," I offered, kneeling in front of her.

Addison rolled her eyes. "I feel like an invalid."

"You're not an invalid," Janet said, having stepped off the ice. "You're carrying a miracle in your belly. Creating a life isn't easy."

"I'm just ready to have my body all to myself," Addison said with a sigh.

Janet patted her shoulder. "I know. Not too much longer, dear."

I finished lacing Addie's skates and helped her to her feet. "How does that feel? Too tight? Too loose?"

"They're perfect," she said with a sincere smile. "Thank you."

She, Janet, and Dad went out to the ice, and I sat beside Willa, who hadn't moved.

After a moment, she whispered, "Sometimes it's weird seeing you together and knowing you have so much history. It can mess with my head, and I hate that because I know you love me. You're not doing anything wrong, but sometimes I do feel like the other woman."

"Even if you and I were not together, Addison and I would not be a couple. Our relationship isn't like that anymore."

She looked at me. "I know. I do. I know it, but it still makes me feel insecure sometimes."

I took her hand in mine. "I know I've put you in a tough spot, but this will get easier."

A grin curled her lips, and she said, "Let's go skate."

We went around several laps before I spotted trouble.

"Oooooh shit!"

Willa's brow lifted. "What?"

I looked behind her. "It's the diarrhea woman. She's here with a group of people."

Willa's eyes shot wide open. "Shut. Up."

I shook my head. "She's coming this way."

Willa laughed and couldn't seem to stop laughing. She was snorting and bending over as tears fell from her eyes. "Oh my God, I'm gonna pee my pants."

"Glad you're enjoying this, but I don't want half the people here thinking I shit myself."

She sniffled, stifling her laughter. "So what you're saying is this really came back to bite you in the ass."

She broke into another fit of laughter, and I couldn't help but smile. Her laughter was contagious.

She put her hand on my chest and swallowed. "Sorry, I'll pull myself together."

Addison and Shelby glided over to us, probably because Willa was making a scene with her outburst. Shelby gave Willa a look. "What's happening over here?"

Willa said, "He told—" Her laughter interrupted her words. "He . . . Diarrhea!" She was back to crying.

Addison and Shelby looked to me. "Did you shit your pants, bro?"

I shook my head. "No, but I told someone I did."

"No, you didn't." Willa corrected, pulling herself together. "You told her you had explosive diarrhea all over yourself and me for some reason."

Addison narrowed her eyes. "What the hell?"

Willa explained, "He was in a hurry and doesn't know how to turn people down quickly without hurting their feelings, so he lied about diarrhea. And now she's here."

Shelby immediately looked around, trying to spot the woman. "Where?"

I glared at Shelby. "I'm not going to point her out. She's here with a big group."

Shelby glared back. "You think she hasn't noticed you over here. Willa's causing a scene, laughing like a lunatic."

Addison put her hand on her belly, and Shelby said,

"See, all this hysteria is even upsetting Addison's unborn baby."

I rolled my eyes. I'd learned a long time ago to take everything Shelby said with a grain of salt. She had always been overly dramatic, but after her ugly drawn-out divorce, that drama had taken on a dark hue of cynicism. I gave her grace, knowing her callous indifference and brashness came from a place of pain. She was meanest when she was hurting.

"You know what? Let's just go skate," I said with resolve. "She might not even remember me."

As soon as I turned and started skating, the diarrhea woman was right there. I almost ran right into her, and she definitely remembered me.

She gasped, her lips peeled back in disgust.

Willa skated between us. "He doesn't really have diarrhea. He just doesn't know how to turn women down." Willa peeked back at me. "We're working on it."

"What the hell is wrong with you people? You're so weird." With that, the stranger skated away.

"Change of plans. Let's go get some hot chocolate," I said, grabbing Willa's hand.

DANCE OF THE SUGAR PLUM FAIRY

WILLA

WE SAT on stools along the side of the rink, drinking our hot cocoa. It was cold, but there was no snow, just the grey bleakness that spoke of winters in this corner of the world. It didn't feel very Christmassy without snow, but there were possible snow flurries tomorrow.

The sky darkened, and as dusk settled, all the string lights above and around us came to life, and suddenly it felt a lot more like Christmas. "White Christmas" played over the speakers, and Oliver took my mittened hand in his and led me out to the ice. As we glided forward, I looked up at him and smiled, feeling immensely grateful to be here with him at this moment, no matter how strange the day had been. He was worth it.

I wanted to kiss him, but I couldn't do that while skating. I pushed him toward the wall of the rink. Oliver's back hit the barrier, and I leaned up on the toe picks of my skates, but before I could land a kiss, Oliver gasped and jerked away, taking off across the ice. I followed his direction and saw Addison sitting in the middle of the ice. Oliver slid to an easy stop and got down on his knees in front of her.

I shoved back my disappointment and skated toward them. By the time I got there, the whole family had flocked to her.

Oliver was on the ice, looking her over, and she seemed irritated, saying, "I fell to avoid plowing into the little kid who darted in front of me. Oliver, I'm fine." She pushed him back. "Give me some space."

"Are you sure you're okay," Oliver fussed.

She gave him a look of exasperation. "I'm sure I'd know if something was wrong. I landed on my knees, not my belly. The baby's fine. I'm fine. Everyone is fine. Now, will you please help me up? My butt is freezing."

Oliver stood and helped her to her feet. "Do you want to go get checked out just to be sure?"

"Oliver," I admonished at the same time Addie chastised, "Oli!"

Janet finished, "She's obviously fine, son. Let it go."

Buck put his arm over Oli's shoulder, leading him away, and I heard him say, "Oh, this is just the beginning. The baby hasn't even been born yet. Just wait until . . ." They left earshot, and dread pooled in my stomach. Everything I worried about just became more real. I wasn't so sure I was cut out for this. The logical part of me could work it out, but living it was harder than I'd realized. There we were about to kiss, and he ditched me without a word to go check on Addison. I understood why he did, but it sure made me feel like she came first.

I believed he wanted me, but how many times would he put her before me? It made me feel small, but I couldn't help my feelings.

When it was just the two of us, everything made perfect sense, but seeing him with his family and everyone else who knew him best made me feel like I was just an accessory and not vital to him in any way. I was jealous of Addison because she seemed to have such a crucial role. One she'd so easily thrown away.

We all filed off the ice, and Oliver helped Addison take off her skates while I sat by myself a few benches over.

After we turned in our rented skates, Oliver found me. He sighed, looking back at Addison.

I said, "Why don't you ride back with Addison?"

His eyes jerked to mine. "Why?"

"Because you're worried about her, and that way, you know she's okay."

"Are you okay?"

I stared at him. "I'm fine. You should go."

His eyes narrowed. "Is that what you want?"

I nodded. "I need to drive around and clear my head. This day has been a lot to take."

He backed up, looking unsure. "Okay." He grabbed my hands. "I love you, Willa."

"I love you, too."

He leaned forward and kissed my cheek before turning back toward the group. I watched as he spoke to Addison. She looked surprised and then turned to look at me. I spun around and walked to our car.

I had to catch my breath. I didn't know if I could do this. I had to stop comparing myself to her. I wasn't in a competition, but it felt like I was competing for attention, and would I feel this way once his daughter was born. The last thing I wanted was to grow resentful of his child. How awful that I was even considering such things.

Everything seemed to be so effortless for Addison. She was only thirty, and she was a doctor, had a house and an apartment in the city. She obviously had no trouble fitting in, and she was pregnant without even trying. Did everything come easily to her? Part of me hated her, but she had tried to make amends for her mistakes. Or perhaps she was manipulating Oliver and me. Maybe she wanted Oliver to herself and was playing some kind of long game.

She'd played Oliver like a fiddle for eleven years, so would he even see it? Maybe she couldn't be trusted. Did she see we were going to kiss and fell on purpose?

My ex-husband had caused me to think the worst of everyone. But I guess when you put that much trust in someone, and they betray you, you don't just stop trusting the person who betrayed you. You stop trusting yourself and, in turn, everyone around you.

Oliver had been a victim of the same kind of broken trust, but he was different. He was overly forgiving. He chose to see the good while I couldn't help but see the bad.

So, were Addison and Oliver's family out to sabotage me, or was I sabotaging myself. Either way, I wouldn't let it tear us apart. No matter what I was feeling right then. The fact remained, I loved Oliver. He saw me better than anyone else, and I saw him. We were great together. Holidays didn't last forever, and this tough time would pass.

I wouldn't give up on Oliver, just like he hadn't given up on me. And I would protect him if Addison was playing some kind of game. She didn't know who she was dealing with. I could fight dirty. When honey badgers are cornered, they don't go for the throat. They go for the genitals. Hit 'em where it hurts the most. And what would hurt Addison more than everyone knowing she was less than perfect. I could ruin her life with the secrets I knew about her. Oliver was too kind to tell anyone that Addison slept with his best friend, but if I found out she was toying with Oliver and me, I'd tell the world her secrets.

WHEN I GOT BACK to the house, Oliver was waiting for me outside. He walked to my car door as I got out of the vehicle.

"Are you okay?" he asked.

I grinned. "Yeah. I just had to work some things out, and I never got to kiss you." I reached up and wrapped my arms around his shoulders while I lifted onto my toes. Our lips met, and my fingers climbed up the back of his neck into his hair while he held me against him.

Our kiss grew heated, and I could feel him growing hard, his length pressing into my abdomen. I reached down to stroke him with my hand over his clothes, earning me a moan.

I panted against his lips, "Can we take this inside, or do you want to go for a car ride?"

His eyes flashed. "Definitely car."

He was already digging the keys out of my coat pocket, and I ran around the car getting in the passenger seat while he sat behind the wheel and started the car. Then we were driving away.

I reached over, stroking him through his jeans. "Do you know where you're going?"

"Yeah, it's not far."

I unzipped his fly and reached in, achieving skin contact. I stroked him, and Oliver inhaled a sharp breath, his spine stiffening.

"Do you want me to stop?" I asked.

He shook his head. "No, I really don't. It just takes a little more effort to drive."

"Are we close?"

"It's just up here." He nodded with his head.

I pulled my hand away. "Then I'll wait."

He turned on the radio, and Christmas music came on. He knew I was sick of Christmas music, so he went to change it, but I stopped him. "It's fine. It makes you happy, and it is Christmas Eve's eve."

As we pulled off the road, Oliver said, "I've never had car sex before."

I leaned back. "Really?"

"Nope."

I loved it when I got to experience things with Oliver that no one else ever had. "Well, let's remedy that."

It was a wooded area, and the narrow road was curvy, but it was a quick trip before Oliver pulled into a small parking area that was nothing more than a clearing with a pine needle floor. He turned off the headlights.

I asked, "Are the doors locked?"

"Yes, and no one can see in the tinted windows unless they're right on top of us," he said, turning to me.

I looked around. "I feel like this would be a great place to get murdered."

"I promise you won't get murdered," he said with a smirk.

We crawled into the backseat, and I straddled him as soon as he sat down, but we were still fully dressed. I moved to the side and stripped my bottoms off while he unbuckled his belt and pulled his own down. Sitting next to him, I wrapped my hand around his very firm shaft and leaned over, taking him in my mouth. It was a beautiful thing, the sounds he made, the taste of him, but my angle was wrong. I pulled my knees up on the seat, so I knelt over him on all fours. It left my ass up in the air, and Oliver took full advantage, his hand skimming over my stomach and sliding between my thighs. His hands were skilled, and his fingers slipped between my folds, finding my most sensitive area, and proceeded to torture me in the best way possible. It was distracting me from what I was doing, but he didn't seem to mind the extra noises he provoked from me.

My thighs shook, and I knew we both needed the same thing, so I climbed into his lap, and his award-winning cock slipped into my sweet spot, sinking deep before my body moved, and I set the pace. His hands fell to my hips while our mouth became reacquainted. I had to keep my head down, or I'd hit it on the ceiling, so I nuzzled in and sucked on his neck.

Oliver lifted me, switching our position so I was lying on my back with him above me. He had one knee on the seat and one on the floor. I braced my hands against the door above my head to keep us from sliding. It didn't last much longer, his orgasm following closely behind mine.

His weight rested on me as we both caught our breath,

and I laughed, "We just orgasmed while listening to 'Dance of the Sugar Plum Fairy.'"

He playfully bit my neck. "This is from *The Nutcracker*, right?"

I nodded, and he said, "My new favorite song, my little sugar plum."

ALONE IN A CROWD OF STRANGERS

OLIVER

On our way back to my dad's, Willa said, "I can't believe we've only been here for a day. It feels like so much longer."

"They do like to pack things in. This is a more relaxing year, too," I said.

"So we're having dinner and then going to see lights?"

"That's the plan."

Willa flipped down the passenger visor, fixing her hair in the mirror. "Your family is going to know that we just had sex."

I shrugged. "So."

Willa let out a nervous laugh.

It was a quick drive back, and when we arrived, Janet and Shelby were setting the dining room table. The dog came running into the room and immediately went for Willa, but I caught him and made him sit. He listened, and I wished Shelby would take the dog for obedience training. He was willing to listen. She just was too flighty to control him.

Willa and I got cleaned up before dinner, and the meal went pretty well. We had pleasant conversations. It wasn't until dessert that things turned. Janet set pumpkin and apple pies on the table, and then she and my dad went to the office to have a video chat with Janet's daughters.

After they left, Shelby said, "This is weird. This whole dynamic you three have going on is awkward."

Addison sighed while Willa's fork paused on the way to her mouth.

I cleared my throat. "Thanks for that very astute observation, Shelby."

"I feel like Willa can't have babies, so she's using Addison as like a surrogate or something?" Shelby set down her fork and looked directly at Willa. "This kid won't have any of your DNA."

Willa's mouth hung open, stunned into silence.

I scooted back and stood, leaning forward on the table. "Shelby, what kind of question is that? Stop being such a bitch."

Her head jerked back at my words. "Aren't you worried she's only with you so she can steal your baby?"

I glanced at Willa, who was still frozen into silence, her eyes shining with unshed tears.

I glared at Shelby. "That's ridiculous, and you know it!"

"Isn't that why she divorced her last man? Because he couldn't give her kids."

I shouted, "Damn it, Shelby! Did you hit your head? What's wrong with you?"

Willa's laughter interrupted my question. Both Shelby and I stared at her, confused by her reaction. She was laughing so hard she had trouble catching her breath, and tears streaked her cheeks.

Shelby made a noise in the back of her throat. "Oh great, another hysterical outburst."

Willa caught her breath and wiped her tears, saying, "Oh, Shelby, I can appreciate you trying to protect your brother, but dear Lord, you are eleven years too late!" She held up a hand to Addison. "No offense, Addie. I really do like you."

Addison looked baffled and glanced at me. I shrugged.

Willa continued, "And Shelby, my ex-husband got his mistress pregnant and felt the right thing to do was divorce me. Have I thought about stealing a baby before? Sure, but only from parents who don't deserve them, and there are so many. But the idea that Oliver and Addison would fit into that category is laughable. So answering your questions: I'm not with Oliver to steal his baby, but I am excited to be in her life. I never want to step on Addison's toes to make her feel like I'm trying to take the role of mother. And to answer the questions you haven't asked, yet. I met Oliver when he and Addison had broken up. I didn't steal him from Addison. She's given us her blessing, and we don't need yours. I don't expect you to like me. I don't really care. But playing all these games and stooping so low isn't a good look for you."

Shelby's mouth hung open. "Uhhh, I'm sorry, did you just say you've thought about stealing a baby?"

Willa rolled her eyes and gave an exaggerated shrug. "I wouldn't actually do it." She pursed her lips, and the smartass added, "Probably."

Shelby's eyes went wide. "You're a psycho!"

Willa smirked. "Why, Shelby, you're getting all hysterical. Do calm down. All this hysteria is bad for Addison and her precious unborn child."

My face fell into my palm. This was turning into a catfight, and they were both bullheaded enough that they might kill each other, and Addison would be a witness.

I wrapped my hand around Willa's arm. "Willa, come on."

Once we were in my bedroom, I said, "You didn't have to provoke her like that at the end."

She folded her arms over her chest, her demeanor shifting to something much more grave. "How did she know, Oliver?"

I stared at her, trying to follow the bread crumbs she was dropping me. I knew the longer I stayed silent, the worse it looked. "How did she know what?"

"That I have an ex-husband. That my marriage fell apart after years of fertility issues."

My eyebrows raised. "I honestly don't know. They knew you were married previously, but I didn't give any details, and I've kept everything else between us."

"Then how did she know?"

"Willa. I swear. I don't know."

She inhaled a deep breath. "This day is going to give me whiplash."

We dressed in layers for the Christmas light show. We'd be walking around outside, so I wanted to make sure we stayed

A SPARKLING CHRISTMAS MOSCATO

warm. When we made it back to the dining room, we helped clean up dessert, and Dad announced, "We're taking the van. I cleared it out so we could all ride together."

The van wasn't something they drove frequently. I didn't even know why they still had it. It was a third vehicle that mostly sat in the garage.

"Why do you still have that thing?"

"It reminds me of when you kids were young, and I figured it would come in handy for lugging people around sometimes."

We loaded in.

Willa and I sat in the very back while Addie and Shelby rode in the second-row bucket seats. Dad was driving, and Janet was in the passenger seat.

Christmas music came from the stereo, so I said, "'Last Christmas.'"

Willa propped her elbow on the windowsill and looked out into the dark. "'Hallelujah,'" she mumbled.

"Oh my god, Oliver!" Shelby spun in her seat to look back at me. "Remember, like four years ago, when the car in front of us broke down at the entrance into the parking lot, and you had to get out and help push it."

Addison spoke up, "Travis and Brad got out to help too. They were so pissed at each other."

I shook my head at the memory. "I'm the only reason Travis didn't murder Brad that night."

"You should've let Travis kill him," Shelby said. "Stupid cheating bastard."

Addison looked to Willa, trying to include her. "It was snowy that year, and Brad was complaining that he wasn't getting out to help push a car because he'd get snow on his shoes, so Travis pulled him out of the car by his jacket."

"He dragged him out, and his ass landed in the snow," Shelby finished with a big smile.

"I stepped between them before Brad started a fight he couldn't win," I added.

Shelby snickered. "Yeah, but they fought anyway. As soon as you turned your back, they were wrestling in the snow."

Addison cut in. "We pulled them apart, moved the car that broke down, and by the time we got in and started looking at the lights, Travis and Brad were wet and freezing from rolling around in the snow."

Shelby leaned between seats. "We had to leave like five minutes after getting there. It was ridiculous. All because my asshole ex didn't want to get snow on his shoes."

Addie noted, "We were literally going somewhere to walk through the snow and look at lights."

I smiled, looking over at Willa, who looked to be attempting a smile. I didn't know how to cheer her up, or even if I could. She didn't believe me, which frustrated me, but if we were both mad, then nothing would get resolved.

Willa looked back out the window, and the remaining conversations went on without her.

The evening had grown colder, and Mom and Harry decided not to come because of the frigid temperatures. We could've opted to do the drive-through light show, but it was tradition to get out and walk through the lights. In the center, they had a Santa for the kids, real reindeer, and best of all, they served hot chocolate and other warm beverages.

The crowds were still thick despite the single-digit weather. Willa shivered, and I wrapped my arm around her.

She didn't pull away, which I took as a good sign. I wasn't used to her being upset with me.

"There's hot chocolate up here," I told her.

"And eggnog!" Shelby added, nudging Addie. "Right, Addie?"

Addison and I both laughed, remembering the time she'd had too many, and I'd had to carry her back to the car.

"So many fun memories," Willa said. "I can see why you'd want to bring me here."

I didn't know how to take that, so I said, "Now, you're part of those memories."

"And just think, next year, you'll have a baby with you!" Shelby chirped.

We walked under a giant arch of lights, and Buck said, "Cady will have to come next year."

"I'll have to put that girl on a leash."

Janet said, "One of those backpack ones? I think that would probably be best for everyone."

Shelby said. "And it's gotta be harder to snatch a kid that's attached to one of those."

"I think those are for kids younger than four." Willa said, "Cady will be able to figure it out and get out of it."

Shelby said, "Well, that sucks! Why do you know so much mom stuff when you're not a mom?"

Willa inhaled. "My best friend has three."

"Oh my, and you couldn't have any?"

I felt Willa stiffen. "Nope."

"You were probably too uptight. You just need to get drunk and sloppy, and it'll happen."

My arms curled tighter around Willa, knowing Shelby's words, no matter how unintentional, hit on a sore spot for

Willa. I was about to say something when Willa took a deep breath and said, "We spent over fifty-thousand dollars on specialists and treatments. We tried for years, but you're probably right. All we really needed was to get sloppy drunk." She pulled out of my grip. "I'll wait at the entrance."

I watched her walk away, glancing at Shelby, who looked shocked and embarrassed.

"God, Shelby. You and your mouth." I shook my head in disappointment before turning to jog after Willa.

When I caught up to her, she was wiping tears with her mittens. "Go away, Oliver. I just want to be alone."

"Alone in a crowd full of people?"

She stopped and turned to me. "Alone in a crowd full of strangers who won't care if I'm crying."

"Willa?"

"No!" She shook her head. "Please, just give me a little time to feel how I feel without you watching me."

I stared at her for a moment before relenting. "Okay."

She walked away from me. I stood there, not sure what to do.

Addison approached. She didn't say anything. She just stood there beside me.

"When did life get so damn hard, Addie?"

"It's always been hard. You simply have a sunny disposition and have lived with your head in the clouds."

I sighed, rubbing a gloved hand over my face. "It's so fucking cold out here."

She nodded. "Yes. It was insane of us to think this was a good idea. The lights, that is."

"Where's the rest of the group?"

She pulled her scarf up over her nose. "Janet took the van keys and ran after Willa. Buck and Shelby are getting drinks, and we're just standing here in the freezing cold surrounded by lights none of us are paying any attention to. I wish I could go straight back to my hotel room and take a long hot shower, but now I have to ride back with this fun group."

My eyes shot to her. "Hotel? I thought you were staying with your parents."

She shook her head. "My dad's still not talking to me. I'm meeting with my stepmom while I'm here, but he told her I'm not welcome at the house."

"Addie," I wrapped my arms around her, pulling her in for a hug. "I'm so sorry. I didn't realize it was that bad."

"You probably shouldn't have your arms around me, Oli." She pulled away, glancing around to see if anyone had spotted us.

I stepped back. "Willa's mad at me." I didn't mean to say it out loud, but since I did, I followed it up with, "She thinks I gave Shelby those details about her."

Addison looked down at her boots. "I didn't know about it. Of course, you didn't tell Shelby." She hesitated, asking, "Are you guys trying to get pregnant?"

"No, it's way too soon for that, but it's a painful subject for her, and she feels like I betrayed her. But I didn't. I never told Shelby anything."

"Could she have overheard you talking to someone else?"

"The only thing I've said is that she's divorced."

"Maybe she guessed."

I sighed. "This isn't going the way I'd planned."

She snickered. "I'm finally learning that things rarely go as planned. That's not always a bad thing." She ran her mittened hand over her round belly.

CAN'T, IT'S TRADITION

WILLA

IT WAS DARK AND COLD, and the wind was brutal next to the parking lot. When I was walking through the crowds, I hadn't noticed it so much, but it was so much colder out in the open. I pulled my scarf up to cover my face, leaning against the brick pillar of the entryway.

I'd ruined the evening, but wow, did Shelby know how to get under my skin. Really, her bitchy personality was only the tip of the iceberg. There was a whole mountain of icy trouble beneath the surface. My distrust, anger, and jealousy had been building all evening.

Addison and Oliver seemed to have such an easy connection. They had so much history, and I felt like it was being rubbed in my face with all their stories and inside jokes. They were able to communicate with just their eyes, and it was hard to watch the man I love have that kind of connection with someone he'd slept with for eleven years.

And Shelby seemed to egg it on. She'd hit so many buttons. I'd just had enough. I felt justified in what I'd said to her, but I'd made it awkward for everyone else. I was so mad at myself.

"Willa?"

I turned toward the voice and found Janet walking toward me. "I have the keys." She held them up, letting them dangle. "Let's go get warm before we lose toes to frostbite."

I nodded, and together, we walked to the van. It wasn't an uncomfortable silence, but I wouldn't call it comfortable either. It was just silence. And if it had to be anyone in Oliver's family, I was glad it was Janet who came to my rescue.

"Sit up front with me," she said, just before hopping in the driver's seat.

I sat in the front seat, and that's when the silence became awkward. Christmas music played quietly, and I took off my mittens and held my fingers over the vent, trying to warm them faster.

"I had four miscarriages before my girls were born," Janet said out of the blue.

When I turned toward her, she was watching me with a calm smile.

"I'm—"

"Don't say sorry," she directed, and I clamped my mouth shut. "Why do we do that? Say we're sorry when what we really mean is I hate that you had to go through that."

I shrugged. "It's a reflex, I guess."

"To be sorry? To constantly apologize for things out of our control? When I heard what you said back there, I didn't feel sorry for you. I felt angry for you. I felt heartbroken for you. My own heartbreak has faded, but hearing yours seemed to pop my memory vault open, and all these feelings came gushing out."

"I'm embarrassed that I said all of that and . . . I hate that it brought up your past."

"I'm not." She reached out, squeezing my hand. "Willa, you're not alone, and sure, there will be plenty of Shelbys who will give you terrible advice thinking they're helping, but there are also women like me who understand."

Just hearing her words validated so many of the things I'd been feeling. It helped me breathe easier.

She continued, "Your history adds another layer of complexity to your relationship with Oliver. I will never force you to talk, but I want you to know I'm here, and I'm a good listener. Even if it's venting about how much Addison is complaining about being pregnant."

"I know she loves her baby," I defended.

"I know. I never said she didn't. But I know how tough it is to listen to someone complain about being pregnant when it's something you'd die for. And before you say it, I know she deserves to complain. But so do you, and there aren't as many people who understand the complexities of what you're feeling."

"Thank you, Janet. This trip has been a jarring experience for me, and your kindness means a lot. I know how it looks from the outside, but Oliver and I love each other."

"That much is obvious." She squeezed my hand again and then pulled it away. "It looks like they're headed our way."

I looked out the windshield, and sure enough, the four of them were nearly to the van.

As I climbed into the back, I grumbled, "This should be awkward."

"Nah," she said. "If I blare Christmas music, no one will be able to talk. Perks of having an old van." She cranked the volume dial and then popped the knob off. She turned and winked at me as she put the knob in her pocket.

The doors opened, and the cold air swept through the van, sending a shiver through me. Janet moved to the passenger seat so Buck could get in, and the rest of us took the seats we had on the way. Oliver climbed into the back with me, looking nervous. As he sat down, I grabbed his arm and looped it over my shoulder, leaning against him.

He kissed the top of my head.

"Oh my god! Turn that down!" Shelby yelled.

Janet swiveled from the front seat. "Can't, the knob broke."

"Then turn it off!" Shelby demanded.

"Can't!" Janet shouted. "It's tradition to listen to Christmas music to and from the lights."

"Ugh," Shelby groaned. "I hate my life!"

EIGHT SPINDLY LEGS

WILLA

I FELT a lot better after talking to Janet, and by the time we got back to Oliver's dad's house, I was ready for bed. I still felt uneasy about how things went down, but being wrapped in Oliver's arms always seemed to subside those uncomfortable feelings.

The next morning started slow. It was only Buck, Oliver, and me. Janet had to work a shift at the hospital but would join up with us in the evening. After a lazy breakfast, we packed up and got ready to go to Oliver's mom's house.

While Oliver assured me Christmas day was laid back and without real structure, Christmas Eve was an event filled day. Kim and Harry had a fancy dinner on Christmas Eve, so everyone dressed in their finest attire. The catered food was served on fine china. They called it Classy Christmas, and Oliver had told me about it beforehand. I only hoped the dress I brought was appropriate.

We packed our elegant attire and our overnight bags into the car before leaving Buck's. We were staying the night at his mom's but would come back to Buck's the following evening. I hated that Janet and Buck would not be with us until the evening for Classy Christmas dinner. They had sort of acted as a buffer, and knowing I would be spending the day with both Shelby and Kim made me nervous.

"Relax," Oliver said, squeezing my thigh on our drive to his mom's. "I'm right here with you."

I nodded and took a calming breath. He had been there last night, and things still went sideways, so his words weren't all that comforting. Oliver couldn't control the way his family behaved, and I didn't trust Shelby.

His mother's house was in a ritzy neighborhood and was much newer and larger than Buck's.

When we arrived, Oliver led me in through the back door. He set our bags by the door and draped our garment bags over a chair as we entered the kitchen. Shelby sat on a high back bar stool at the breakfast bar with a mug wrapped between her palms. She was wearing pajamas with her hair piled on top of her head. She had bags under her eyes and glared at us when we walked in.

"What happened to you?" Oliver asked as he helped me out of my coat and pulled out a bar height chair for me. It was at the breakfast nook, which was part of the immensely oversized island in the most elegant kitchen I'd ever set foot in. It looked like the kitchen from a cooking show. Absolutely beautiful.

"Brad happened to me," Shelby spat, vaguely.

Oliver's brows lifted, and Kim walked into the kitchen, saying, "I got Cady back to sleep." She noticed us and walked over. "Good morning, my handsome son." She hugged him, placing a kiss on his cheek. "And, Willa." She hugged me, and I pretended not to be surprised.

Oliver sat between Shelby and me. "I thought Cady was staying with her dad."

"Her dad dropped her off early this morning," Kim answered in a calm tone as she leaned back against the counter. "She's napping. She didn't get much sleep last night."

"Neither did I," Shelby complained. "That bastard told her Santa wasn't real! Then dumped her on my doorstep when she was inconsolable. She cried all morning."

"Why would he do that?" I questioned.

"Because he's an asshole!" Shelby shouted.

Kim answered more calmly, "He said it was an accident. But his story kept changing."

"It's probably so he could get all the credit for the gifts he bought her," Shelby huffed.

Fluffy ran into the kitchen with a chewed up shoe in his mouth. Shelby saw it and screamed, "That's my Jimmy Choo, you fucking bastard!" She jumped off her stool, and Fluffy wagged his tail like she was playing. As soon as she lunged for him, he took off into the other room and Shelby followed.

Kim closed her eyes and took a breath. "I swear if she wakes up that child, I'm going to wring her neck."

"Has Shelby been staying here?" Oliver asked.

"She only stays here when Cadence's nanny is off. Brad doesn't want split custody of Cady anymore, but Shelby can't seem to do it on her own and keep up with her blog, so we hired a nanny to help."

"I didn't know."

"She prefers it that way."

"But she's still working?" Oliver asked.

"Yes."

"Can't she afford to pay for her own nanny?"

"I like being able to help my children. You'll find out soon enough. You'll do anything for your child."

"Knock knock," Travis said as he and Addison walked in the back door.

Fluffy ran up to greet them with the shoe still hanging from his mouth. "You little bastard!" Shelby shouted.

Before Shelby reached them, Travis said, "Sit."

Fluffy sat.

"Drop it."

Fluffy dropped the shoe.

Shelby slid to a stop and threw her hand back in preparation to slap the dog, but Travis caught her wrist, saying, "Acting hysterical isn't going to make your dog listen to you, and hitting him won't make him understand."

"What are you? The dog whisperer." She jerked her arm out of his grip and gave him an evil look. She reached down and grabbed the shoe, waving it in Travis's face. "These were twelve-hundred dollar shoes!"

Travis snorted. "That's your fault for spending twelve-hundred dollars on shoes!"

Shelby was shaking, her face turning red. She let out a frustrated shriek and stomped out of the room with the damaged shoe in hand.

Everyone was staring at Travis, who bent down and scratched Fluffy's head.

Harry came into the room, wearing a brown tweed jacket

with the elbow patches. He had a rolled-up newspaper under his arm, and I half expected him to be carrying a pipe. He ran a hand over his slight comb-over and slid his wire-framed glasses off his face as he said, "What's all the commotion?" He set the newspaper on the counter, pulled a handkerchief out of his pocket, and started cleaning his glasses.

Kim sighed. "Shelby's having an unpleasant morning."

"Oh." He slid the glasses back on his face. "Addison, Travis, nice to see you." He nodded. "Oliver." His eyes slid over me without acknowledging my presence before he picked up the paper and left the room.

Oliver stood, grabbing our bags. "I'm going to put these in my room."

"Okay, but be quiet," Kim warned. "Cady's sleeping in there."

"Nuh-uh!" Cady said from the kitchen entrance. She lurched forward. "Auntie Addie! Did you know Santa's not real?"

Addison knelt down to be the same height as the little girl. "Who told you that?"

"Daddy."

"Well, it sounds like Daddy's been on the naughty list one too many times," Addison said, "Of course, he doesn't believe in Santa. That doesn't mean Santa isn't real."

"But he said the elves and reindeer aren't real, either."

"Well, I've seen reindeer with my own eyes. I can tell you for a fact that they are real."

"Really?" Cady asked.

"Yep."

"So Santa might be real, too?" Cady asked. She looked up at Travis. "Do you know if Santa's real, uncle T?"

Travis stooped down but shook his head. "Who else would've put me on the naughty list?"

Her eyes rounded. "You're on the naughty list?"

"Afraid so, munchkin." He tousled her hair.

She smiled and turned to Oliver. "Uncle Oli, do you believe in Santa?"

He smiled. "Of course I do."

She looked at me. "And you?"

I nodded, and she said, "Mommy's right. Daddy is a bastard."

Travis snorted while the rest of us tried not to laugh. Oliver coughed to cover his laughter and choked out, "I gotta take these . . ." He left the room with our bags.

Kim stepped toward Cady. "But remember, name-calling isn't nice. It can get you put on the naughty list."

Cady said, "Are you on the naughty list for calling Oliver's friend a gold-digging whore?"

Kim froze. "Uhh, where did you hear that?"

"I heard you and grandpa Harry talking." Cady turned to me, walking toward my chair. "I wanna be a gold-digging whore. Do you get to keep the gold?"

I opened my mouth to say something. Maybe defend myself, but then tilted my head to the side and grinned. "I get to keep *all* the gold."

Her eyes widened. "Really? Is it the kind of gold with chocolate inside?"

Now, that's my kind of girl. "It sure is."

She climbed up in my lap. "Did you eat too much chocolate, and that's why your skin looks like chocolate milk?"

I laughed. "Not exactly. I was just born this color."

She ran a hand down my arm. "It's pretty. Do you think if I eat chocolate, my skin will be like yours?"

"I don't think so, but your skin is pretty just like it is."

Kim said, "Cady, come with me. We need to get you ready to go." Cady hopped off my lap, and the two of them walked out of the room. Addison came over to sit next to me, but Kim popped back in, saying, "Addison, would you help me get Cady ready?"

Addison stood up. "Sure."

Travis sat down next to me. "Don't worry. I've been called worse things."

"You were never sleeping with their son," I responded.

"Nope. Not their son."

I looked at him, and he shrugged.

I looked out the window. It'd been trying to snow all morning. There was a flurry of tiny snowflakes dancing through the air that never seemed to touch the ground. I sighed. "I have thick skin."

He scoffed. "I never doubted that. I know you're tough."

I didn't like the way he said it, as if he knew me. I looked at him. "We aren't the same."

He smirked. "Hallelujah for that, right?"

My eyes narrowed, and he grinned, grazing his knuckles against the counter. "Welcome to the family." He knocked on the counter twice and left the room.

I stared after him, and a few moments later, Oliver came back in, saying, "We're getting ready to leave for the toy drive. I guess Shelby is going to skip it. She needs some rest."

I nodded. "Oliver, did Travis and Shelby ever—"

"No!" He laughed. "God, no!"

"Okay."

"Well . . ." he paused, looking worried. "At least I don't think so. Why?"

"Just a comment he made."

He shook his head. "No, no, I'm sure he hasn't. He was probably messing with you."

Harry poked his head in. "You two ready?"

"Yeah. We'll meet you there."

Travis walked into the room, saying, "I'm coming with you guys."

"Oh. Okay."

WE SPENT the next few hours helping with the toy drive before breaking for a late lunch of Chinese food, which, I learned, was another family tradition. Afterward, we met back at Kim's house, where we spent the next couple of hours gathered in the family's movie theater room watching *Home Alone*. We sat on the tiers of reclining couches, all aimed at the monstrous flat screen.

Cadence, who now decided I was her best friend, fell asleep on the sofa between Oliver and me. I judged the kid too soon. She was a sweetheart under the layers and layers of dysfunction her parents were instilling. I was nodding off by the time the movie was over. Then it was time to get ready for family photos.

We changed into our formal clothes, which meant a long shimmering hunter green dress for me and a charcoal suit with a dark green tie for Oliver.

I stood in the floor-length mirror, my shimmering green pumps looking perfect with the dress and giving me some extra height. Oliver walked up behind me, and together we looked impressive. I spun to kiss him.

Pulling back, I admitted, "I feel way overdressed."

"You aren't, and you look gorgeous in that dress."

I held his hand while I twirled in a circle. "And not a feather in sight."

He laughed, leading me out to the formal living room, which I hadn't yet seen. It looked like a beautiful window display of Christmas. Every inch decked out in holiday decor, looking like the backdrop of a Hallmark Christmas movie.

Everyone's stockings hung on the mantel. Even Travis and Addison had one. I walked forward, and Oliver said, "I'm gonna go grab us some drinks. We'll need something strong to make it through all these pictures."

I nodded, concerned. That was saying something coming from Oliver. My eyes scanned the fireplace mantle, taking in all the beautiful decorations. My fingers glided over the ornate stockings.

"We have one for you," Harry said, coming up from behind me.

I spun to him. "Oh."

He reached behind the Christmas tree and held up a cheap felt stocking with my name scrawled across the top in permanent marker. The ink had bled into the fabric to look blotchy and uneven. "We'll put it up later. It's too ugly to hang with the others during pictures. We wanted to include you for Oliver's sake, but we aren't going to go to the trouble of having your name embroidered until we know you're sticking around. You understand."

I raised an eyebrow at his bluntness. "Of course, I understand," I said. "Should I hide for the pictures, too, so you won't have to edit me out later?"

Maybe he didn't understand my sarcasm because he said, "No, we'll make sure to take some pictures without you so that won't be necessary."

My eyebrows folded together. Perhaps he had a really dry sense of humor. "Are you kidding?"

He shook his head. "No. Why would I joke about that? It makes the most sense to get pictures with and without you. If Oliver decides he wants to stay with you, then you'll have photos from your first Christmas, but if Addison and Oliver get back together, it'd be awkward having you in all the Christmas photos. It would just remind them of the time they spent apart."

He said it very matter of fact, and I guess he maybe had a point, but it was an incredibly insensitive thing to say. I couldn't tell if he was being a dick on purpose or if he was always brutally honest and a little socially awkward.

Harry stuffed my stocking back behind the tree and walked away.

I tried not to let him get to me, remembering I had thick skin. I would not let them chase me out of Oliver's life.

He came back with our drinks, two glasses of amber-brown liquid. "I was getting you a glass of wine, but Travis said it would take something stronger to get through family photos. I think he's exaggerating, but Addison agreed with him. This is bourbon." He held the drink out to me. "You don't have to drink it.

"I'll take the bourbon," I said, grabbing the glass and taking a drink. I held in my wince, asking, "Is Harry awkward?"

"I wouldn't call him awkward. He's very analytical. Maybe a little standoffish."

"Does that come across as being kind of rude?"

He looked concerned. "I guess it could. Why? What happened?"

I shook my head. "Nothing. It's not a big deal, just the way he spoke about the pictures."

Oliver's shoulders slumped. "He goes overboard with pictures. We'll be here for a while, and he'll get every combination of people. It's irritating, hence the alcohol."

EVERY COMBINATION, indeed! As afternoon melted into evening, we were still posing. Cady had gone to take another nap, and I wondered if I could do the same. I don't know where they found the photographer, but this obviously wasn't their first time dealing with this family.

Currently, Addison was standing in front of the tree, and they were getting pregnancy shots.

The photographer called, "Now let's get the dad-to-be in the next picture."

Oliver moved to stand by Addison.

The photographer directed. "Put your hands on her belly."

Oliver gave Addison a look, and she said, "It's fine."

He tentatively placed his hand on her stomach and jerked it away before his face lit up and he pressed his hand tighter against her belly, exclaiming, "I think I felt her hand!"

He started talking to her belly, pressing his face against it. He'd felt the baby move before, but not this much. She seemed to be doing a little jig inside Addison's belly. The rest of the family was mesmerized by the moment, rushing forward to touch her stomach while she stood there looking like an angel in her ice-blue dress. It was a sweet moment, but one that gnawed at my confidence.

I looked away, noticing Travis across the room. He reclined back in an oversized chair, with one ankle on his knee. The dog was sleeping on the floor beside him. Fluffy had been following him around all day and he hadn't seemed to mind.

Travis chewed at his nails, something I'd never seen him do before. As if sensing me watching, his eyes flicked to me, and he dropped his hand. We stared at each other, both of us appraising the other. He looked away first, blowing out a breath like it was painful being here. Then I remembered what they'd said about his family.

I closed my eyes, taking a deep breath. I wouldn't let anything get to me. I was titanium. It didn't matter if the family forced Oliver to kiss Addison. He was going home with me.

Shelby came and sat by me. "You're wrinkling your dress."

"I don't think they need me for more photos," I said.

"No, probably not, but I'd want to look my best if I were you."

I looked at her. "I don't think a few wrinkles makes much difference."

She didn't look at me. She was staring at Addison and Oliver. "She is beautiful, isn't she?"

"Yes, she is."

"I wouldn't want to compete with that," she said conversationally.

I clenched my jaw. I needed another bourbon. "Good thing no one is competing."

"Mommy!" Cady ran into the room, up from her nap.

I used the distraction to make a run for it. I needed to be alone for a moment so I could catch my breath.

As I walked toward the bathroom, I heard my phone ringing from Oliver's bedroom. I grabbed it just in time. "Hey, mom."

"Willa, your dad and I were just sitting here missing you, so I thought we'd call to see how it's going."

I felt the tears clog my throat and swallowed. I missed them too. I closed the bedroom door for privacy. "Mom, I wanna come home. I miss you and hate being away for the holidays. Especially when that means being here with all these awful people."

"Oh, honey, I hate you being away from me too, but Oliver is important to you. If you're going to spend your life with the man, you have to be able to tolerate his family."

I let out a breath. "I know, but they all think I'm a home-wrecking, gold-digging whore who has him pussy whipped. You know all those Hallmark movies where the girl takes home the big city guy to meet her parents in her small town, only to realize she's still in love with the small-town boy. I feel like I'm in some warped version of that scenario, and everyone is rooting for me to fail."

The door opened, and Oliver came into the room with purpose. He picked up the baby monitor in the corner and flipped it off.

My mouth fell open, and my eyes widened, feeling a

wave of sudden rolling nausea in my stomach at the realization. "Shit, mom. I've gotta go. I'll call you back later."

Oliver looked pissed. "What the hell, Willa? Everyone's been nice today."

My eyebrows rose. "Nice? You call what's been going on, nice?"

"You called my entire family awful."

I shook my head. "I was generalizing, but most of them are awful. This is the worst holiday I've ever had, and last year I caught my husband sleeping with his mistress, so that's saying something."

"I'm trying to make this work, and so is everyone else. Why can't you give a little?"

I gawked at him. "The only thing they're trying to *make work* is you and Addison!"

"Nobody is trying to do that! Except maybe you."

Anger crept up my spine like the eight spindly legs of a cellar spider. My anger felt like poison, and I wished I was something more deadly—something feared, like a black widow or a brown recluse. Something that could bite and rid itself of the venom, but I was not even a real spider. I was a daddy long leg, delicate and without defense. And Oliver's family knew it. They'd been plucking my legs off one at a time, and I had to get out while I still had legs left to stand on.

"All of those things I said on the phone are true. They didn't come from my mouth. They came from your family. And can we talk about why there's a baby monitor in your room and why it was on?"

"Shelby uses it for Cady. She was just taking a nap in here because it's the closest bedroom to the family room."

"She uses a baby monitor for her five-year-old?"

"Yeah. That girl will straight color the walls with a permanent marker. We have to keep an eye on her."

"And why didn't you turn off the other monitor when you heard me talking?"

"Shelby had it. She probably wanted to finish hearing what you really thought of the family."

I took a step back. "If you don't see the problem there, I'm not going to explain it to you. I've taken everything they've thrown at me, Oliver, but I can't take you not believing in me."

"My not believing in you?" he said with anger. "You're the one who accused me of telling my sister all your secrets."

I shook my head. "Maybe you didn't do it on purpose but—"

"Willa, I didn't tell her!"

I grabbed my purse. "I'm going to go for a drive to clear my head." I walked past him and out of the bedroom. The family was gathered and waiting to pounce in the family room. It was the only way out unless I jumped out a window, which I seriously contemplated.

But I was a motherfucking honey badger. I held my chin up, rolled my shoulders back, and walked through the room, relieved I didn't see Cady.

Shelby approached. "Willa, if we've been harsh, we're sorry. We're protective of Oliver."

I turned on her so quickly, she jumped. "First, where is your daughter?"

"Outside with Dad and Janet."

"Good!" I said, but groaned inwardly. I'd make an ass out of myself in front of them once again. Too late now, I stepped toward Shelby. "Shelby, you're full of shit. You made up your mind about me before I arrived, so as long as we're not worrying about feelings, let me give you some advice. Your daughter is sweet as pie, and she needs you to be a parent, not a father bashing, spiteful bitch. She admitted to me that she'd manipulated her dad into getting her a dog, and she's working on getting another. And you really can't handle that. Within five minutes of meeting you, Cadence ruined my favorite sweater, and your dog humped me so hard that he ripped my favorite pair of leggings, and instead of apologizing, you shrugged. You need to get your house in order and if you can't handle the dog, give him to someone who can. You're only teaching your daughter to be irresponsible and manipulative." I looked around the room. "And the rest of you who watched everything happen without saying a word, shame on you."

"Willa!" Oliver used my name as a reprimand, pulling on my arm, but I yanked out of his grip and spun on him.

"And you!" I poked his chest. "I didn't want to come here, but you promised it would be okay. You promised you wouldn't leave my side, and you immediately broke that promise." I shook my head. "I wanna believe in us because what we have is great, but you threw me to the wolves, Oliver. And the worst part is you don't even see it."

I went for the exit with tears clouding my vision. I didn't know if they were angry tears or sad tears and figured it didn't matter. I felt betrayed. I grabbed my coat from the closet, which slowed me down, but it was necessary.

"Willa," Oliver said, coming after me. He stepped in front of the door. "Willa, wait."

Addison stepped into the room. "Willa, can I please talk

to you?" I looked back over my shoulder at her. Her face was a mask of concern, but I was done listening.

I shook my head. "I have no room left to listen." I pushed Oliver aside and brushed past him, saying, "He's all yours."

I ran out the door and to the car without even putting my damn coat on. It's okay. My anger was keeping me warm.

PACK OF WOLVES

Oliver

I turned in the door to follow Willa, but Addison stopped me, saying, "Let her get some air."

I hesitated, and she said, "She was right about everything. Except for you being all mine. Neither of us wants that."

I turned toward her, and she nodded her head to the side, toward the room off the foyer. "Come here." I followed her into a side room, which Harry had recently turned into his office even though he retired years before.

Addison closed the glass doors and said, "You once told me Willa was a pistol, and you weren't kidding. That woman is a loaded gun, and with the beating she's taken the last couple days, it's a miracle she didn't go off sooner."

I scrubbed a hand over my face. "I don't know what happened. I love her, Addison, but I don't know."

"Oh, Oli, I'm going to give it to you straight. Your mom and sister are class A bitches."

My eyes jerked to her. "What? You always got along with them."

"I love them, but I know how to play their game because I'm a bitch. I know how to speak their language. Willa doesn't play those games. She was right when she said you fed her to a pack of wolves. You just didn't realize they were wolves."

I ran a hand over my face. "Fuck."

She walked to the door. "Sorry to leave you with that, but the way I pulled you in here, they're all going to think we're getting back together, and we can't have that." She turned and left.

I leaned against the desk, going over everything in my head. My sister could sometimes be a bitch, but she was harmless, and my mom was sweet and professional. Wasn't she?

I stepped out of the office, walking toward the family room. I stood out of sight in the hallway and listened to what they were saying.

Shelby whispered, "She's practically unhinged."

"It's better he sees it now than months down the road," my mom added.

I stepped out of my hiding spot, and all heads turned toward me. "Is that what you think?"

Mom and Shelby exchanged a glance while Harry's expression stayed blank. Travis was sitting at the edge of the sofa in the corner. Addison leaned against it. My dad walked into the room in a black suit while Cady and Janet were absent.

I stepped forward. "I begged her to come here with me and meet all of you because you're the most important people in my life." I shook my head. "I've never been more disappointed in my family."

"In us!" Shelby said. "What about you?"

I spun on her. "What about me?"

"Come on, Oliver. Addison is having your baby. The two of you belong together. We figured if we could get you together, you would see that."

I was speechless.

Luckily, Addison wasn't. "This isn't a Hallmark movie, Shelby. Just because we're back in our hometown doesn't mean the magic of Christmas is going to bring us back together. We still care about one another, but we're adults, and together, Oli and I ended our relationship. The end."

"But your history—"

"Is just that," I said, regaining my voice. "History."

"But she'd take you back," Mom said. "Wouldn't you, Addie?"

Addison's eyes widened. "Oh wow!" She pushed away from the sofa, saying, "No. I wouldn't."

There was a long period of quiet where Addison and I exchanged an exasperated look.

Addison continued, "No, I won't take him back because I'm not in love with him, and he's crazy in love with Willa."

"You could get that love back," Shelby said. "Look, we all know I made a mistake with my douche of an ex-husband, but Oli is one of the good ones. And so are you."

Addison huffed in frustration and then shot me an apologetic look before confessing, "I cheated on him." She took a breath, and I closed my eyes for a moment while Addie contin-ued, "He didn't want to tarnish my reputation or for anyone to blame me for our breakup, especially while I was pregnant with his child. But I cheated on him. He's forgiven me, mostly because if it hadn't happened, he wouldn't have found Willa. She's the person who helped put him back together after I blew up his life, so stop blaming her for anything. They belong together. Not us. Stop trying to put us back together."

The quiet in the room was palpable. Shocked faces exchanged glances before Travis broke the tension by raising his glass and toasting, "Happy birthday, Jesus!"

As people thawed, there were a few small laughs, and several people took long drinks of whatever alcohol they had in hand.

Shelby shook her head as she looked at Addie. "Why in the world would you cheat on him?"

Addison winced. "I don't know. I was stupid and reck-less. It was years ago and I was confused."

I was grateful Addison hadn't thrown Travis under the bus with her. It was no one's business. And apparently, my family held ugly grudges.

Shelby started, "But—"

I stepped forward. "It's in the past. I've forgiven her."

Shelby turned to me. "You clearly haven't if you're no longer together. Not saying you should be together. But if it's between Addie and Willa, Willa doesn't seem like she even likes kids. She got all freaked out when Cady got her shirt dirty. Newsflash! Kids are gross."

I sighed. "She likes kids, Shelby. She's a teacher."

Shelby snorted, "Poor kids."

Okay, the gloves were off. I stepped toward her. "Shelby, that's enough! I'm done with your attitude."

She sucked in a breath, gawking at me.

I wasn't one to lose my temper, but I was done. "She wasn't upset Cady got her shirt dirty. She was upset because that was her favorite sweater, and she was trying desperately to make a good first impression. Especially after she heard you and mom call her a homewrecker. And she wouldn't even let me yell at you for it."

Shelby rolled her eyes, and I stepped forward. "I love you and my niece, but I'm not the only one to question your parenting style. You have a right to be bitter for what Brad did to you, but your bitterness is turning you and your daughter into monsters. Just because you're hurting doesn't give you the right to be rude and insensitive to everyone around you. I've given you so much grace, and for what? You've been unbelievably heartless to Willa. You owe her a huge apology."

Shelby looked pissed. I turned to the rest of the group, clarifying, "You all do. Don't worry. I plan to spend the rest of my life with her, so you'll have plenty of time to figure out your apologies."

I left the room, going to my bedroom to retrieve my phone so I could call Willa and grovel.

I held my breath as the phone rang, worried she wouldn't pick up. "What, Oliver?"

"Willa, I'm sorry. You were right. Please come back."

"Oliver, I—" Her gasp almost covered the squeal of tires across the pavement. Her scream was met with a sickening crunch and shattering glass before the call disconnected.

"Willa. Willa!" I shouted uselessly into the phone.

Travis showed up at my side in the hallway, and I couldn't remember leaving my room.

"Oli, what's up?"

"She screamed. I think she got into a car accident while I was talking to her."

I dialed her number, and it went straight to voicemail. I hung up and did it again three more times. "Maybe she's trying to call me." I stared at my phone, waiting for it to ring, but after several moments, I decided she wasn't trying to call me. I called her again.

"There are some shoddy reception areas around here," Travis said. "Could be that."

I looked at him. "She screamed."

"Umm."

I rubbed a hand over my forehead. "I just need to know she's okay."

"Don't jump to conclusions. Do you know where she went? Does she share her location with you?"

"Yes!" I pulled the phone from my ear. "She shares her location." I pulled it up. "Shit. There's nothing."

"What's going on?" Addie asked, walking toward us.

"Something happened to Willa," I said.

Travis filled her in. "Willa's call disconnected in the middle of her screaming."

"Oh!" Addison paused. I watched her mind work. "Where would she have gone?"

"I don't know. She doesn't know this area."

"But normally, what would she do if she was mad at you?"

"She'd call her mom," I said as I hit her mom's number.

She answered right away. "Hello, Oliver."

"Have you spoken to Willa?"

"I was just on the phone with her. She switched over to take your call, and then I figured she forgot about me and hung up."

"Do you have any idea where she was headed?"

"Didn't you talk to her?"

"Yeah, but we got disconnected." I didn't want to worry her until I knew more, so I stayed vague. "Reception is spotty in some areas around here."

"She was going back to your dad's house to pack. I like you, Oliver, more than I ever liked Evan, but you better fix this, or I'll hunt you down. I won't watch my daughter's heart break again."

I was already walking for the door. "I'll fix it. I promise. And thank you for your help."

"Don't make me regret it."

I hung up, and Addison and Travis had stuck with me, so I explained, "She was on her way to my dad's."

Travis shook his head. "Which way? There are multiple ways to get there."

We were walking through the family room when Janet stopped us. "What's going on?"

I said, "They can explain. I've gotta go."

Addison followed me, demanding, "I'm going with you. We can take my car."

Travis called after me. "Which way are you going?"

"The back way," I said over my shoulder. "It's how we drove here."

"Okay, we'll split up. Keep your phone on."

We grabbed our coats out of the closet, and we were out the door.

CALLING OUT INTO DARKNESS

TRAVIS

OLIVER HAD BEEN TERRIFIED, and if Addison hadn't insisted on driving him, I would have. After I explained what happened to the family, we split into teams of two and covered different routes.

Buck had friends on the police force here, so he called them to report what Oliver heard and see if they had any accidents matching the car she was driving. The police had nothing, but they sent some patrol cars to check out those areas. It was a twenty-minute drive between his parents' houses, and it'd been thirty minutes since Oliver had talked to Willa.

All of us arrived at Buck's a few minutes apart. By the time we got there, Oliver was pacing the driveway, his hands interlinked on top of his head. Addison was on the phone with the hospital, checking to see if anyone matching Willa's description had been brought in.

I sat in Shelby's car, idling in the driveway. Cady was in the backseat, thinking we were playing a game.

Addison hung up her phone and walked to Oliver. I jumped out of Shelby's car to hear what Addison had found out.

"It doesn't sound like she's there," Addie said.

Oliver blew out a breath, looking relieved, but then he sunk down. "What if she's out there hurt or dying alone all because I let her down?"

Addie put her hand on his shoulder. "You're jumping to conclusions. We don't know anything yet. Don't go directly to the worst-case scenario."

I sunk to his level, looking him in the eye. He didn't look good. He was pale and scowling, which looked unnatural for him. "Come on," I encouraged. "We do another pass. We don't stop looking."

He nodded.

"Breathe, buddy. We're gonna find her."

He swallowed and inhaled a deep breath. "Okay. Yeah, let's go." We stood, and he added, "We'll backtrack the same routes. I'll tell the others."

I shook my head. "No, you guys go. I'll let everyone know."

I sent out a quick group text, letting everyone know the plan. That way, if one of us found her, we could relay it to everyone faster.

The flurries turned to heavy snow, and I groaned. Of course, it was snowing. Any other time I would be happy for snow on Christmas Eve, but the snow made it harder to spot any tire tracks.

Cady was in the backseat wearing headphones, listening

to a movie on her tablet while Shelby complained, "I freaking hate driving in the snow." She sighed, and more quietly asked, "Why do you think she did it?"

"Willa? Because—"

"No," she interrupted. "Addie. Why would she cheat on him? I always thought they were the perfect couple. I looked up to them."

I exhaled, searching out the passenger window as I answered, "Do we ever really know what's going on inside of someone? The more perfect they appear, the better they are at hiding their flaws."

"But I know Addison," she argued.

I glanced at her. "Do you?"

She sighed, and I looked back out into the night, searching.

In a small voice, she said, "You already knew about it, didn't you?"

I nodded.

"And you're still friends? You still rode here with her after knowing what she did to your best friend. After knowing she's a cheater."

"That's not all she is," I said to the window. "People aren't just one thing, Shel. You're not just a mom. People are fucking complicated, no matter how perfect they appear. Everyone has hang-ups and insecurities. I know she didn't set out to hurt your brother, and I know the guilt eats at her." It was the same way it ate at me.

She muttered, "It's just a lot to process."

I understood that but there was more she needed to consider, so I continued, "Willa has changed Oliver. She taught him to stand up for himself. Something I've been trying to teach him for twenty-six years. She's tough but not hard, and she must love him. Otherwise, she wouldn't have put up with any of the shit you guys have put her through."

Cady started mumble-singing to music we couldn't hear. Shelby was quiet, looking intently at the road. I let my words sink in as I continued my search for anything out of place.

Snow accumulated on the road, and the car moved forward at a crawl. It gave me more time to scour the dark roadsides, which is how I noticed the area where the long grass was flattened, and snow lay smoother. It didn't quite look like tire tracks, but it could've been and it was such a steep drop that she'd be completely hidden from the road at night.

"Shelby, pull over!"

"Here?" She questioned. "I can't. It's too steep of a drop."

"Put your flashers on."

"Travis, my baby is in the car. I'm not stopping on the road. I'll pull over up ahead."

"Just let me out and then go park up there."

"Uggh, fine." She stopped the car, and as soon as I hopped out, the car was moving again.

"Dammit, Shel!" I slammed the door just before it was out of my reach.

Then I was calling out into the darkness. "Willa!"

I rushed through the snow, backtracking to the area we passed. I pulled out my phone using the flashlight, although it seemed pointless through the thick snowflakes.

"Willa!" I called again as I got closer to the matted grass.

"Yes! I'm here! Down here in the ditch!"

"I'm coming down." I dialed Shelby. When she

answered, I said, "Shelby, text the group. Call Oliver. Tell him we found her." I hung up and slid the phone into my pocket. I went to the edge of the steep grassy slope. It had to be at least twelve feet down and at the bottom was a densely wooded area. I slid down and immediately spotted her. I jogged forward, relieved that she was standing on her own.

"Are you hurt?"

"Umm, no, just a little shaken up." She stepped forward, still wearing her heels with a coat over her silky dress. She had her arms wrapped tightly around herself, and I figured she had to be freezing. She'd been out here for almost an hour.

When I got closer, I realized there was blood on her face. "Your face is bleeding."

She shook her head. "They're shallow cuts. Nothing serious."

I stared at her, starting to get angry. If she was okay, why the hell didn't she come up the slope and try to flag someone down. Didn't she know she'd freeze out here? I looked at the car. Though she hit a few branches, the car didn't look like it was in terrible shape.

I turned back to her. "Are you sure you're okay?"

Her nod was a little wooden. "The airbag didn't deploy, but the branch broke the windshield and umm . . . almost . . ." She blew out a breath as tears filled her eyes. "I heard cars passing by, but I just couldn't get my legs to hold me."

"Are they hurt?" I asked, opening the driver's side door and ducking down to take a look inside. And holy shit! The branch that came through the front windshield was as thick as my thigh and went all the way through to pierce the back seat. If it would've been six inches to the side, Willa wouldn't be here right now. I turned around and pulled her into a hug that seemed to surprise her. I knew I wasn't her favorite person but that didn't matter right now. I heard her sniff and knew she was probably in shock.

When I pulled away, I looked her over again. "Are you sure you're okay?"

She took a shaky breath and swallowed. "I think so. I mean, I have my head, so I'm doing a lot better than I could've been."

"Oliver's already losing his mind. He can't see this. At least not tonight. We gotta get you out of here."

"Travis!" Shelby yelled.

"Yeah!" I shouted back. "I've got her. I'm bringing her up." To Willa, I said, "I'm going to text the group our location."

"Group?" she asked.

I looked at her and then back to the car, closing my eyes at how badly it could've gone. "Yeah. Everyone is out looking for you."

"Really?"

"Yep, even Shelby. Oliver made a whole speech about how they need to apologize, and they'd have plenty of time because he plans on spending the rest of his life with you. It was all very dramatic. Hell, maybe we are in a fucking Hall-mark movie."

She laughed. "I think you just proved that we're not by using the f word."

It was good to hear her laugh and joke. It helped reassure me she was okay. And I really needed her to be okay for Oliver's sake.

My phone rang and I picked it up, "Hey, man, did Shelby call you?"

"Yeah. Is Willa okay?"

"She's alright. I just sent you the location. Here she is."

I handed the phone to Willa.

"Hey, I'm okay. A deer ran out in front of me, and I swerved. The roads were slick, and I slid into the ditch. I'm fine."

I rolled my eyes. She almost died because of a deer.

She was quick on the phone, and when she hung up, I said, "Next time, hit the fucking deer."

She shrugged. "It was a reflex." She eyed the steep incline where I came down and then looked at her feet. "I don't know if I can make it up there."

Under the trees, we were mostly shielded from the snow accumulation, and the bed of pine needles covering the ground was so thick that it minimized the underbrush. "Shelby parked down that way." I pointed parallel to the road. "I think we can walk through the woods until we get to her car. It's not as steep of a drop where she pulled off."

She gave me a hesitant smile. "You lead the way."

DR. BOSSYPANTS

Oliver

Addison put her flashers on and pulled off the road to park right behind Shelby. I jumped out of the car and didn't see them. Shelby got out of her car, saying, "They haven't come up yet."

"Where are they?" I asked, my anxiety rising.

She pointed toward the woods. "That way."

My feet itched to move, but there were no footprints to track. I'd be moving aimlessly. I pulled out my phone, calling Travis.

Willa answered, "Hi."

"Where are you guys?"

She hesitated. "We're on our way."

"Is everything okay?"

"I mean, this isn't how I saw my Christmas Eve going, but umm . . . we're fine. Travis says we're almost there."

"Okay." I hated just standing there. I needed to do something. "Do you need me to get anything out of your car?"

"No. I have my purse and I think my phone is busted. Everything else is at your parents' houses."

"Okay."

"Oliver, take a breath." She inhaled deeply, and I mimicked her, breathing deep and blowing it out.

"God, Willa. I was so scared," I whispered.

"I know. Me too."

I saw a shadow moving through the snow, and I stepped forward, the phone still held to my ear. I expected two shadows but only saw one. I realized why once they got closer.

"For the record. I was against this, but it really was the safest and fastest way to get to you," Willa said, and I heard her voice through the phone and in person.

I hung up and rushed forward. Travis held Willa in his arms, cradling her like a bride. Irrational anger pummeled me even as she tried to joke. "The heels and dress aren't ideal for a hike through the snowy forest."

I pulled her out of his arms and held her against me in a crushing embrace. She wrapped her arms around my neck, burying her face in the crook of my shoulder. Her skin was freezing.

"Easy man, don't crush her," Travis said.

"I know what I'm doing," I said, even as I eased my grip. To her, I whispered, "Let's get you in the car where you can get warm." Her hold on me hadn't lightened up, and I felt her warm breath on my neck as her body shivered.

Addison stepped out of the car, saying, "Travis, you drive. I want to look her over."

"Okay," he said, "but she'll be fine until we get back to the house."

"I want to know if she needs X-rays."

Willa shook her head, whispering, "I don't want to go to the hospital. I'm fine." She looked at me, her eyes begging. "Please, Oliver. I just want to go home."

"Addison, she's fine. You can look her over at the house."

She didn't seem to like that but stayed silent. She opened her trunk and took out a foil blanket. "Wrap that around her," she said, laying it in the backseat before getting back in behind the wheel. Travis told Shelby to go on without him, and as she pulled away, he got in the passenger seat of Addison's car.

I loaded Willa into the backseat and slid in next to her, pulling her into my lap. I took off her heels and wrapped the blanket around us. The ride was quiet with muted conversation between Addison and Travis. Willa and I were mostly silent as we held each other. She didn't stop shivering the entire way back to my mom's house. At one point, she asked, "How did you guys know where to look for me?"

I said, "Your mom told me where you were going."

"Did you tell her what happened?"

I shook my head. "No, but we should call her later."

Once we got to the house, Addison turned into Addison Arthur MD and ushered us to the master bathroom. I carried Willa even though she told me she could walk.

As soon as we got to the bathroom, Addison said, "Run a bath with lukewarm water for her to thaw her feet. Too hot, and it will feel like it's burning."

She sat Willa on the vanity seat, claiming it was the best light. "You have superficial lacerations on your face." She pointed to the counter. "I need that makeup light to get a better look. Travis said the windshield broke."

I handed her the light while Willa said, "Yeah. My face was bleeding. Travis made me wipe it off before Oliver saw me." She looked at me. "He said you'd freak out."

He wasn't wrong, and I was already freaked out.

Addison said, "Travis shouldn't have done that. You could've pushed the glass in deeper." She shined the bright magnifying mirror light in Willa's face. "Oliver, hold the mirror, and hand me the tweezers."

"Yes, doctor," I said to her demands. I grabbed tweezers from the counter, and Addison wiped them with the cotton ball of alcohol. She looked at me. "Hold it higher, please."

I held it higher, saying, "You know, the blue nylon gloves almost matched your ice blue dress. Makes a real statement."

Willa winced as Addison pulled something out of her face. "You had a pretty big splinter in your cheek." She held it up for us to see. Looks like wood." She had her thinking face on, finally asking, "How did the glass break?"

Willa bit her lip. "A branch came through the windshield."

Addison stared at her, waiting for more, but let it drop when it was apparent she didn't want to talk about it. "Did the airbags deploy?"

"No."

"Do you have cuts, scrapes, bruises anywhere other than your face?"

"My arm."

"Will you show me?"

I helped Willa out of her coat, and she said, "I didn't put

my coat on until after the accident." She looked at me. "Will you unzip my dress?"

The hunter green dress did a good job hiding the blood, but her dress sleeve was ripped at the bicep. I unzipped the dress halfway down her back, and she slid her right arm out of the sleeve.

Addison inspected it. "You could use some sutures, but I know you don't want to go to the hospital, so I can use steri strips to tape it together, but it might leave more of a scar. Do you have a history of keloid scarring?"

Willa stared at Addison. "What now?"

"Keloids."

Willa looked confused, and Addison said, "That's a no then."

"What the hell are keloids?" I asked.

Addison didn't look up as she sorted through the medical supplies. "It's a raised scar caused by excess collagen while the skin is healing. Some people are more prone to getting them."

Willa raised an eyebrow. "You make me feel dumb sometimes."

Addison said, "I have that effect, but really, it's just medical stuff." She ripped open a package. "I would make a terrible teacher."

"I doubt that." Willa hissed, squeezing my hand as Addison started cleaning the wound.

Once Addison finished taping the wound closed, she covered it with a bandage and instructed, "Try to keep this dry for a bit." She removed her nylon gloves. "I'll go get some plastic wrap to tape around it so you can shower." She dipped her hand in the water I'd run and said, "Go ahead and soak your feet in here while I get the plastic wrap. Also," she dried her wet hand on a towel, "I'm going to write you a prescription for antibiotics, so you don't end up with an infection."

She left the room, and Willa looked at me. "She's kind of a Doctor Bossypants. Don't get me wrong. I'm grateful that she's so good at telling people what to do."

I laughed. "Oh, she's a Doctor Bossypants for sure."

SNOWFLAKE PAJAMAS

WILLA

OLIVER STAYED with me while I soaked my feet and showered. And he was there when someone knocked on the bathroom door as soon as I finished blow-drying my hair. I was wrapped in nothing but a towel, so Oliver cracked the door, blocking me from view. I heard Kim's voice. "These are for Willa."

"Where did they come from?" Oliver asked.

"They're a gift."

Oliver took whatever it was she had, saying, "Thank you." He closed the door and set the snowflake pajama set on the counter.

I ran my hand over the soft, cozy material, dying to put them on. I picked up the long sleeve shirt and smelled it. "These look brand new, but they smell freshly laundered."

"My mom always gives us new, already washed, pajamas on Christmas Eve so we can wear them Christmas morning."

I held the shirt against my chest. "She bought a set for me too?"

He gave a grin. "It's official. You're part of the family now."

I smiled, feeling the warmth of acceptance spreading through me. His family had come out to search for me, and now this.

Oliver interrupted my happy thoughts. "Or maybe I should call it a wolf pack." His smile melted and he took my hands in his. "Willa, I'm so sorry."

I swallowed. "I could've handled things better, and I should've been open instead of trying to deal with it all by myself. Travis said you lectured them after I left."

He nodded. "Yeah, once I got my head out of my ass and realized you were right. It helps that Addie told them she cheated on me and that you're the one who put me back together."

I inhaled. "She said that?"

He nodded.

I shook my head. "I still don't understand why she wouldn't fight for you. I would fight for you if I were her. Why would she give you up?"

He smiled. "Thanks for making it sound like I have no say in it."

"Just saying. I would try to win you back."

"Do you want Evan back?"

"NO."

"Don't you think I wonder what moron would let you slip away so easily? We've both been with people we thought were our forever people, but I don't want Addison back any more than you want Evan. And while it's awkward because

Addie is still my friend, she's not pining after me because I wasn't the right person for her."

I took a breath and nodded. "Travis said you told your family you were planning to spend the rest of your life with me."

"I'm starting to think Travis has a big mouth. Do you have a problem with spending your life with me?"

I shook my head. "I want to spend my life with you, but . . ." I swallowed. "I don't know that I'll ever want to get married again."

"We have the rest of our lives to figure that out." He leaned in for a kiss.

I pushed up on my toes to kiss him. When I pulled back, I picked up the PJs and asked, "Will you go get my undergarments from my overnight bag?"

"Sure. I'll be right back."

He left, and I looked at myself in the mirror. My bicep had a bandage over it, and I had a few minor scrapes across my face, but things could've been a lot worse.

There was a knock at the door, and thinking it was Oliver, I said, "Come in."

The door opened, and Addison slid in with my overnight bag in her hands. "I told Oliver I'd bring this to you. His dad needed to talk to him. I hope you don't mind."

I was just glad he gave her the whole overnight bag instead of handing her my bra and panties. Addison turned her back to me, her nose practically to the door. She still had her gown on and looked regal, without a hair out of place. Some things really didn't seem fair.

"I won't look." She said, "You can change, but I need to say some things to you while I have you cornered."

I gawked at her, but she couldn't see me. Who wouldn't want to change in front of their boyfriend's ex-wife? But she'd been nothing but kind, and I owed her an apology. "I'm sorry that I looped you in with the rest of them earlier."

"Oh, I don't blame you. I love Oli's family, but they can make anyone crazy," Addison said.

It surprised me to hear it from her. I dug through my bag and slipped my panties on under the towel.

Addison continued, "Oli is the sweetest man I've ever met, but also completely oblivious at times. His mom and sister can be vicious, and you were right. They were trying to put Oli and me back together, but we set things straight after you left. I told them I cheated and that you were the one to help Oliver pick up the pieces I'd left behind."

I continued to get dressed, unsure of what to say, but it turns out she wasn't finished. "Willa, I know this must be difficult for you. Honestly, it's not the easiest for any of us, but I think we're all adjusting and making compromises in order to make this work. I'm not trying to come between you two. And for what it's worth, I've never seen Oli stand up to his family the way he did tonight. He would fight to the end for you, and I think you should know that."

"You can turn around."

She spun to face me, and I said, "I know Oliver loves me, but sharing him with you is hard." She tried to interrupt, but I held up a hand to stop her. "I can't compete with you, Addison, and I really don't want to, but there are little things that nag at me. You have a history together. His family loves you. You're having his baby. I know how important you are to each other, and I'm not against your friendship. It's just hard not to be jealous of you sometimes. Especially of your connection."

She gave me a sad smile. "Oliver is special, and he doesn't know it. If he were anyone else, neither Travis nor I would be here for his family Christmas, and your life would be a lot more simple, but Oliver doesn't give up on people. T and I are essentially strays that followed Oli home from school one day, and once he invited us in, he's never been able to get rid of us. The three of us became a family, albeit a dysfunctional one, but we don't give up on one another." She wiped a tear and looked to the ceiling. "Wow, pregnancy has made me soft."

"I think soft is a good thing," I said, handing her a tissue.

She dabbed at her eyes and said, "I'd really like for us to be friends, Willa. Honestly, you're probably the closest thing I have to a girlfriend, which *is* as pathetic as it sounds."

Her tears made her seem much less intimidating, and I was a sympathy crier, so if she didn't stop, I'd start. "It doesn't appear that you're going anywhere, so we might as well become friends," I said with a smirk.

She sniffed and dabbed at her face one last time before tossing her tissue in the trash. She peeked at herself in the mirror before returning her attention to me. She smiled her perfect Miss America smile, and it's like she'd never shed a tear. "Come on, let's go join the others."

"Oh, I think I'm just going to bed. I can't go to a Classy Dinner like this."

She rolled her eyes and grabbed my wrist. "Don't worry about it." She pulled me along with her, and I wasn't so sure I was ready to face everyone. Luckily, we ran into Oliver first. He'd changed into pajamas similar to mine, just more masculine. *Oh, my heart.* He was going to wear them to the fancy dinner as a show of solidarity.

"Oh good," Addison said as she passed me to Oliver. "She was going to hide in the bedroom." Addison winked, and then she was walking away, back toward the bedrooms.

I looked at Oliver. "What was that?"

He slid his fingers through mine with a shrug, saying, "Let's go eat."

"Oliver, I really appreciate what you're trying to do, but we can't go in there looking like this. The pajamas were a kind gesture, but let's leave it at that tonight. I can't handle anymore dirty looks."

Oliver tilted my chin up, his touch delicate. "Willa, do you trust me?"

"That depends."

My response seemed to amuse him. "Well, trust me with this. Please. If you're uncomfortable, we'll leave. We can even go back to my dad's if you want."

I watched him for a moment, finally conceding. "Fine."

Together we walked into the empty family room. He pulled me through it and down the hall into the formal dining room. I sucked in a breath, covering my mouth. The table was still made up with fine china and crystal glasses. Steaming dishes were spread across the table, family-style. But instead of gowns and suits, every single person was rocking their own festive Christmas pajamas.

I swallowed, turning back to Oliver with tears in my eyes. I whispered, "I can't cry in front of them."

He shrugged. "Sure, you can."

"Aunt Willa!" Cady said, jumping out of her seat to hug

me. "Look, our pajamas match." She pulled on her shirt. "We both have snowflakes."

It was an overwhelming and dramatic way of showing their acceptance. I leaned in toward Oliver. "Was this your idea?"

He shook his head. "I wish I could take credit, but I was too worried about you. Dinner was the last thing on my mind."

If it wasn't his idea . . . "Then whose idea was it?"

Oliver shrugged, ushering me to my chair. As we sat down, Travis leaned over, saying, "If that's not a fucking Hallmark moment, I don't know what is."

"Let's eat. I'm starving," Buck said.

"We have to wait for Addison," Kim said.

"I'm here," Addison said, rushing into the room in her pajamas. "Sorry, I had a little trouble with the top fitting over my belly."

Her button-up top was hanging open, and she had a tank top on underneath. "Let's eat."

"We have to pray!" Cady complained.

Buck grumbled, and Shelby elbowed him.

"Can I do it, mommy?"

"Go ahead. Keep it short, okay."

She sucked in a deep breath, and I knew it was going to be long-winded. "Dear God, thank you that we found Aunt Willa before she freezes and thank you for the presents we get to open tomorrow and the candy canes and keep Santa safe and warm on his sleigh and thank you that I got to spend the whole day with Mommy and Grandma Kim and Uncle Oli and Uncle T and Auntie Addie and Grandpa Harry . . ."

She was going around the table, and she said mommy twice.

"And thank you that Grandpa Buck and Grandma Jan could be here. And thank you for the food. And I hope there will be lots of snow tomorrow so I can build a snowman and angels and—"

Shelby whispered, "Wrap it up, Cady."

"And thank you for our new jammies, and thank you for everything else. Amen. Let's eat!" she yelled.

The dishes were passed, and everything was delicious. We quickly realized it was far more comfortable to gorge ourselves while wearing pajamas versus restricting gowns and suits.

AFTER EVERYONE STUFFED THEMSELVES, we all retired to the family room where we lounged around, playing games with classic Christmas movies playing in the background.

During this time, Kim gave me a heartfelt apology, admitting she was wrong about me.

Next, Buck approached me with Janet nudging him forward. He said, "I guess I could've done better."

I'm not sure he even knew what he was apologizing for, but I wasn't expecting an apology from him.

I shook my head. "Buck, you don't owe me an apology."

"Yeah, I do. I could've shut Shelby up sooner. I could've realized it was a bad idea to go to lights in one vehicle."

"I don't blame you. If anything, I feel I owe you an apology. You tried to bring the family together, and I made things tense."

"Well, why don't we call it even," he offered.

I nodded. "Sounds good."

Janet came forward, and Buck walked away. "How are you feeling?"

"I'm okay."

She pulled me in for a hug. "I'm glad you're alright." When she pulled away, she said, "And I'm sorry I didn't do more to help you yesterday morning. I was distracted and flustered. I've had problems with Shelby and Cadence not following the rules in my house, and I was trying to bite my tongue until Buck got back. I don't want to be the evil step-mom, but they tend to bulldoze right over me. I realize that has to change, and that has nothing to do with you, but I wanted you to understand why I didn't do more to help you."

I gave her another hug. "I'm so glad you're here. And I don't know how anyone could think of you as an evil step-mom. You're a godsend."

Oliver walked over, his arm around Shelby.

Janet smiled. "Well, I'll let you guys talk."

Shelby moved out of Oliver's grip. "Oliver said you wanted to know how I knew about your history. The truth is, I didn't. I did a lot of guessing." She sighed dramatically. "Yesterday afternoon, when Cady was playing games on your phone, she accidentally closed it and couldn't figure out how to get it back, so she came to me to fix it. When she handed me your phone, your Facebook app was opened, and I was curious, so I looked at it until Cady got impatient, which took all of like ten seconds. All I did was see the list of private groups you were a part of. It's not like I did a lot of poking around, but after seeing the fertility and divorce support groups, I kinda put it together. I'm sorry. It was wrong of me to poke around in your business, I didn't trust you, and I guess I judged you before I even got to know you.

I'm protective of my little brother. Sue me." Oliver cleared his throat, and she amended, "I mean, I'm sorry."

Realizing that was the best I would get, I said, "Thanks for driving around looking for me."

She shrugged. "I never wanted you dead. I just thought you were in the way of Oli's happiness, but I realize that's not the case, so I'll butt out."

That felt like more of an apology than her bogus, "I'm sorry."

I grinned. "Thanks, Shelby."

She didn't move, and I glanced at Oliver.

"I know you both think I'm a bad mom, but I'm doing the best I can. Being a single mom is hard, and how am I supposed to tell Cady her dad only wants to see her one weekend a month. She won't understand." Tears shimmered in her eyes. "He's the selfish asshole, and somehow I'm the bad guy. You guys don't know what it's like. I don't always feed her candy and sugar, but it's been a really rough time, and I'm angry and overwhelmed all the time. I might not be perfect, but I love her with my whole heart and will never give up on her like her father has. So at least that's something." A tear trickled from her eye, and she said, "Great, now Addison's pregnancy hormones are making me cry."

I laughed as I wiped my own tears. "I think they're getting to all of us."

Oliver hugged his sister, and she started crying in earnest. I gave them space, hoping she could release some of the overwhelming feelings she'd been holding onto.

Harry approached me, and I was instantly nervous. He cut straight to the point. "I think our dinner should've stayed formal, but we changed our tradition in an effort to make you feel more comfortable. Based on your reaction, I presume our efforts were a success, so I'm not sure my apology is necessary. Still, in any case, if you misconstrued any of our previous interactions as being unkind, you have my deepest apologies. Emotions are not my strong suit, so forgive me if I've offended you during your time with us."

It sounded so sarcastic, but I suspected it was as genuine as I could expect from him. I still didn't know how to respond, but it turns out he wasn't looking for a response. After he walked away, I mumbled, "I appreciate the effort, I guess."

We had dessert and watched *How the Grinch Stole Christmas*, the original. By the time it ended, everyone was half asleep, and it was time for bed.

OLIVER WAS fast asleep beside me while I stared up at the ceiling, then turned to face Oliver. After my fifth time flipping over, trying and failing to find sleep, I sat up.

I couldn't stop picturing that branch coming through the windshield. The noise it made as it punctured the glass would replay in my nightmares. I never could find my phone, but it had been sitting in the console, and the branch tore the console apart. I could've been torn apart too. It was a matter of inches. I blew out a breath and got out of bed. My body was beginning to ache from the accident.

I threw my robe over my PJs and walked toward the kitchen. I'd grab a drink or some medicine or maybe a midnight snack and go back to bed and dream of sugar plum fairies.

As I walked through the family room, I heard voices. I rounded the corner into the kitchen and found Addison and Shelby alone at the breakfast nook. They looked up at me from their seats as I entered.

Addison said, "You couldn't sleep either?"

"You'd think after this evening, I'd be sleeping like a baby, but nope. I thought you and Travis left?"

"We did, but then we came back. We wanted to wake up with everyone. To do that, I have to fall asleep, but I needed a snack first."

Shelby snickered, "She's living on the edge with her hummus and carrots."

I smiled, asking, "And Shelby, why are you up so late?"

"You and Oliver, plus Addison's pregnancy hormones, made me dig up all the emotions I successfully buried deep, deep down. Now I can't sleep because I'm processing my life. Plus, I took a three-hour nap while all of you were out volunteering this morning."

"And what are you drinking?"

"Vodka cranberry. Do you want one?"

"Sure."

"Coming right up." She turned and went to the fridge.

I asked Addison, "Do you have a room upstairs? I haven't been up there, but Oliver said there were bedrooms up there."

"There are three rooms. Shelby and Cadence both have a room, and Travis and I are in the guest room."

"I told you. You could stay in my room," Shelby offered.

"I'm not going to take your room. It's not a big deal. There are two beds in the guest room. Travis already has the mattress pulled out of the sofa."

"I'm just saying, if you were in my room, maybe I could get lost and accidentally stumble into his bed."

Addison smirked. "Since when are you interested in Travis?"

"Oh, I'm not interested in Travis," she clarified, and Addison and I exchanged a confused look. Shelby went on, "But I still wouldn't mind stumbling into his bed in the middle of the night for some fun."

"Shelby, stop pretending anything has ever happened between us," Travis said as he entered the kitchen.

Shelby turned to him. "Oh, but you forget that we once kissed for seven minutes in heaven."

"And you slapped me when I tried to cop a feel."

"You were my little brother's friend. I wouldn't have even let you kiss me if it wasn't part of the game."

I asked, "How old were you when this happened?"

Travis pointed at himself. "Uh, I was twelve. She was fourteen or fifteen."

"Shelby!" Addison said with mock outrage.

Shelby held up her finger. "First of all, fuck you guys! And second, he did not look like he was twelve, and I was definitely only fourteen."

"Is that the only time you two—"

"Yes," they said in unison.

Shelby said, "Oliver got weird about it."

"Weird, protective?" I asked.

"No, like he wanted us to get married so Travis would be part of the family," Shelby said.

I laughed. "That doesn't surprise me."

Shelby set my drink in front of me and turned to Travis.

"But we could always mess around without letting Oliver know."

"That sounds like an awful idea, Shel. Friends with benefits doesn't work."

Addison stood suddenly. When we all looked at her, she said, "I swear, Emerson is using my bladder like a trampoline." She rushed out of the room, and we all looked after her.

"Travis, would you like a drink?" Shelby asked.

"Nah, I'm going to bed. Good night, ladies." He skewered Shelby with a look. "I better not wake up with you in my damn bed."

She snorted. "Don't flatter yourself. I'm not actually that desperate."

"Night," I said as he walked away. To Shelby, I said, "Would you really sleep with him?"

"Nah, that'd mess things up, but he is fun to look at and fantasize about sometimes. But the moment he opens his mouth, the fantasy is over."

I laughed. "I'm gonna go grab some socks. My feet are freezing."

As I walked through the family room, I heard whispering. My steps slowed.

"Travis, let's just drop it, okay. Obviously, we're not getting anywhere. It's fine," Addison hissed.

"I fucking hate the holidays," I heard Travis say.

"Just run off to go fuck one of your girlfriend's then," Addison said in a hushed voice. I didn't know what to do. If I went back to the kitchen without socks, Shelby would wonder why, but if I kept moving forward, they would know I'd overheard them.

"Are you fucking serious, Addie?"

"Does this one know you're not over your ex?" she accused.

"Jesus, Addie, you're such a bitch."

"And you're a fucking dick," she said back.

I started backing up. I'd take my chances with Shelby. I walked back into the kitchen, and sure enough, Shelby said, "Where are your socks?"

"Um, I didn't want to wake Oliver."

"Are you kidding me? Oliver could sleep through a marching band walking through his room."

I knew this about him. Shit. "Yeah, I know, but it's a new place, and I don't want to trip over anything." Oh, wow, that was lame.

Shelby's eyes narrowed. "Do you want me to go get them for you?"

Addison walked back into the room, and I said, "Nope, I'm just being crazy. I'll go get them." I hurried out of the room.

Travis was still standing in the spot where they'd argued. His face was in his hands, and though it piqued my curiosity, I wasn't about to get involved. I tried to walk as noisily as I could, but I was barefoot walking across carpet, so I started patting my hands on my thighs like that was normally how I walked through a new house in the middle of the night while everyone slept. The only thing that would have been more obvious was if I stared at the ceiling and whistled a tune.

At least it got his attention, and he looked at me. I pretended to be surprised at his presence. I wasn't a terrible actress, but I was awkward in uncomfortable situations.

"I thought you were going to bed," I said.

"And I thought you were having a drink in the kitchen."

I pointed at my feet. "I need socks."

He stared at me, and I walked around him.

"It's not what you think," he said.

I spun to face him, playing dumb. "What isn't?"

He watched me for a long moment before saying, "Nothing."

I nodded. We had an understanding. "Night, Travis."

I grabbed my socks from the bedroom and slipped them on. Travis was gone when I made my way back out to the kitchen.

Addie and Shelby were talking when I entered. By looking at Addison, I doubted anyone would be able to tell she had just had a heated argument with Travis. I wondered if she compartmentalized things or if she usually hid her genuine feelings. Either way, she needed a stiff drink, and because that wasn't an option, I grabbed a cookie tin from the counter. I recognized it from Janet's stash. I took the lid off and slid them on the counter in front of Addison. "I can't watch this anymore. It's Christmas Eve, and you're eating entirely too healthy. Please have some cookies. These are vegan. Janet made them."

She smiled up at me. "Thanks, Willa."

"Don't thank me yet. It's actually a bribe. I was hoping you two could help me with something for tomorrow."

SPARKLING PINK MOSCATO

Oliver

WILLA WAS NOT A MORNING PERSON, so at six am when I rolled over and found her spot empty, I worried that something was wrong. I hopped out of bed and went in search of her.

I heard voices coming from the family room. When I got there, I found Willa and Cady sitting on the floor, cutting up construction paper. They were both still in their pajamas, and Willa had an apron around hers. I paused in the mouth of the hallway to listen.

"Do you want me to cut the middle part with my sharp scissors to get it started?" Willa asked Cady, who seemed to struggle with her safety scissors.

Cady handed the white construction paper to Willa, who made a few cuts and gave it back so Cady could do the rest.

Cady asked, "Can I use the glue gun?"

"We'll do it together, but we have to finish these first."

I stepped into the room. "Merry Christmas."

"Uncle Oli!" Cady turned and jumped up from her spot, running at me. She opened her arms to hug me, but I bent and picked her up, spinning her as we hugged. It drew a giggle out of her, and she said, "Uncle Oli, come see what we're making."

I carried her over to Willa, who was watching us.

"I see Christmas suddenly turned you into a morning person," I said.

"Not quite." She smiled and stood while I set Cady on her feet. Willa walked into my arms and kissed me. Pulling away, she said, "Merry Christmas."

The oven timer went off, and Willa said, "Cady, why don't you show him what we've been working on?" Willa handed me the sharp scissors, whispering, "Protect them with your life."

She left, and Cady held up pieces of paper they had already cut. "We're making props for the photo booth."

"The what?"

She grabbed my hand and tugged me into the formal living room. Sure enough, in the corner, there was a photo booth of sorts with a cellphone tripod and softbox lighting that one would expect to find in a photography studio. The backdrop was a mix of coordinated wrapping paper stacked in squares with bows to look like gift boxes. Attached to it was a seven-foot-tall wreath that started at the floor.

"Where did all this come from?"

"Willa said Mommy and Auntie Addie helped make it. And now I'm helping."

When had they had time to do all of this? I went to the

kitchen to find out. When I got there, Willa was setting freshly made cinnamon rolls on the counter.

She looked up when she noticed me. "Do you want some waffles? I was thinking of making some."

I noticed the empty mixing bowl on the counter. "Exactly, how early did you get up?"

She looked at Cady and said, "Why don't you color the candy canes. Once you're done, we'll start gluing them to popsicle sticks."

Cady nodded and rushed out of the room. Willa noted, "That girl is so excited about the hot glue gun, and I'm getting a little worried."

I gawked at her. "Willa, did you go to bed last night?"

She nodded. "Yeah, I went to bed the same time you did. But then I laid there for almost an hour tossing and turning, so I got up and found Addison and Shelby in the kitchen. Addison and Travis stayed here last night."

"Where'd you get the stuff for the photo booth?"

"Shelby ran home to get the lighting equipment and tripod. I guess she uses it to take pictures for her blog. Anyway, while she did that, Addison and I cut a few branches from the row of arborvitaes out back. We didn't leave any bald spots. We took just enough to put together the wreath. When Shelby got back, she found the wrapping paper and bows. And then we put it all together. We painted a Merry Christmas sign too, but it's drying in Harry's office."

I couldn't believe everything she was telling me. "Addison and Shelby helped with all this?"

"Yeah, but they both pooped out on me when I started making props and mixing the cinnamon rolls. I caught Cady sneaking into the living room at five this morning, so I roped her into doing crafts with me. She's really excited to get her picture taken."

"So you spent half the night working with Addison and my sister? Shelby?" Yesterday they hated each other. I knew Shelby apologized, but Willa wasn't usually so quick to forgive.

"Don't look so surprised. I can forgive people too, you know. We got along just fine last night."

"Grandma!" Cady yelled from the family room.

Willa smiled. "Yay, people are waking up."

"Don't count on that," I said, knowing we rarely got started before nine, but this year there was a level of excitement that hadn't been there before, so I didn't know what to expect.

Fluffy came running through the kitchen, wagging his tail and sniffing both Willa and me before Travis walked into the room in boxers and a t-shirt. He rubbed the back of his neck as he yawned. "Why the hell are so many damn people awake at six in the morning?" He walked to the back door and opened it for the dog.

My mom walked into the room, "Travis, why are you in your underwear?

"I didn't know half the damn house would be awake at six AM, and it's too hot to sleep in those PJs. I was just taking the dog out."

"Go put some clothes on. We'll take care of him."

While Travis left the room, Mom said, "Willa, Cady was telling me about the photo booth. Where did you come up with that idea? It's so clever."

"Thanks. It was a collaborative effort."

"Well, it's wonderful, and it smells delicious in here."

"It's the homemade cinnamon rolls. We have them every Christmas, so I thought I'd make some. I still have to ice them. I thought I'd make waffles once everyone was up. I found a waffle maker in the cabinet. I hope you don't mind that I took over your kitchen. It's a fancy kitchen."

"I'm glad you're using it. We don't use it nearly enough."

Willa added, "I just made a fresh pot of coffee."

That explained the energy.

"Thank you, Willa." Mom turned to give me a look. "She's helpful to have around."

Willa beamed, and I wrapped my arm around her. "I plan on keeping her."

"Willa!" Cady called from the other room.

"Oh, duty calls." She snatched the scissors from my hand and went to join Cady.

Mom said, "I'll ice the cinnamon rolls."

"Thanks," Willa called from the other room.

Fluffy barked from outside, and I opened the door to let him in. "Oh, we got more snow."

"Snow on Christmas morning. It's a holiday miracle." Shelby said in a flat voice. She was still half asleep with her hair piled on top of her head and makeup smeared under her eyes. "I need coffee."

Mom said, "Willa just made a fresh pot."

Shelby swung a look to me, saying, "That woman of yours is crazy. I thought Addie was bossy, but Willa broke out her teacher's voice and put Addison to shame."

Addison walked in. "I smell food."

"Why are you both up?" I asked.

"Freaking Travis!" Shelby complained.

Addison filled in. "He stubbed his toe when he came

back upstairs from letting Fluffy out. He let out a string of expletives that woke us both."

"Is he okay?" I asked.

Addie yawned. "I checked it. I doubt it's broken, but he stubbed it pretty good. I'm supposed to be getting him ice, but those cinnamon rolls are calling my name."

Mom put a freshly iced roll on a plate and held it out to Addie, warning, "I think they have milk and eggs in them."

She snatched the plate, practically salivating. "I don't care."

I said, "I'll get the ice."

AN HOUR LATER, everyone, including dad and Janet, sat around the tree. The gifts stacked beneath spilled out several feet, but the stockings always came first. Willa was near tears when she saw her name embroidered on a plush hunter green stocking.

Mom said, "It's the best we could come up with under the circumstances, but we'll make sure to have a better one for you next year."

"How did you get it embroidered overnight?"

"We got the stocking last night on our way home, after Travis found you. But I had to hand-stitch your name. Don't look too closely. It's far from perfect."

Willa smiled at her stocking. "I disagree. It is perfect. I can't believe you'd do that for me."

They exchanged a meaningful smile that I felt in my gut.

After we finished unpacking our stockings, Cady opened a few of her gifts. I couldn't stand it any longer. I got up and grabbed Willa's gift. Travis had kept it safe for me. And by safe, I mean from me giving it to her sooner.

I set the knee-high box in front of her. "I need you to open your gift."

She laughed. "You need me to?"

"Yes!"

"Okay." She pulled the box toward her. "Oh, it's heavy!"

She looked nervous as she removed the wrapping paper and used scissors to cut the tape. She folded back the cardboard flaps and peered inside. Her body froze—her face unreadable.

"Well, what is it?" Shelby asked. "Pull it out."

I was nervous. What if it wasn't the right one? What if she hated it, and I'd put her on the spot? She pulled the ugly toy nutcracker out of the box.

Shelby gasped. "Oh my God! That's the ugliest thing I've ever seen. It's sooo—"

"Perfect!" Willa finished.

"What is it?" Shelby asked.

"My grandpa used to have a nutcracker just like this, but it was destroyed in a fire when I was young." She looked at me with her head shaking, her eyes aglow. "How in the world did you find this?"

I was thrilled she liked it as much as I'd hoped. "I asked your parents if they had any pictures of it. They had a few. Then I scoured the internet and found nothing. So I asked Travis to see if he could find it and Ta-Da!"

She glanced at Travis. "Is this what you brought over that day?"

"Yep."

"And you took it with you so he wouldn't give it to me ahead of time?"

"Yep.

"Thank you, Travis."

He nodded, and Willa looked back at the toy. "Does it play music?"

"Yeah." I moved forward to show her, and the nutcracker started spinning in circles as the music played."

Willa covered her mouth, letting out a little giggle before her eyes started clouding up. "You're going to make me cry two days in a row."

When the toy finished singing, she said, "I have something for you."

She got up and pulled the bag out from under the tree, handing it to me. I pulled out the tissue paper and bottle. "Champagne?" I asked, and then I read the label. "Sparkling Pink Moscato."

"The label peels back," she said.

I held it up and pulled back the label. Underneath was the outline of a key with the question. Will you move in with me?

I looked at Willa. "Really? Are you sure?"

"Yes, and there's no actual key because you already have the key, but you never stay at your apartment. It's collecting dust, and it's an extra expense for no reason. We can turn the office into the nursery for Emerson. I have plenty of closet space, and I love you and hate it when you're away."

"You don't have to talk me into it." I pulled her to me, kissing her in front of my entire family. When we pulled apart, I said, "Of course, I'll move in with you."

Cady singsonged, "Uncle Oli and Willa, sittin' in a tree, KISSING."

Shelby ignored her daughter, asking, "Does this mean we can celebrate by making mimosas with your pink champagne?"

Willa smiled, and I handed the bottle to Shelby.

The rest of the gifts were exchanged, and we used the props that Cady and Willa made and took a group photo in front of the elaborate homemade backdrop. Willa made waffles for breakfast, and we even fit in a few games before the football games started.

Willa wasn't into sports, but she'd told me at Thanksgiving that she enjoyed having games on in the background. So as I sat and watched a game with my dad and Travis, Willa came and stretched out on the couch next to me. She tucked the throw pillow against my thigh and settled in. I combed my fingers through her hair, and a moment later, she was fast asleep.

The din of laughter came from the other room, making me feel cozy and warm. That, and I had the other half of my heart sleeping in my lap. I could get used to this feeling of happy contentment. It was a bone-deep kind of happy, like a restful sigh had settled over both of our souls.

ACKNOWLEDGMENTS

Thank you to all my readers who said they wanted more Willa and Oliver. I really enjoyed writing this novella.

To my unofficial assistant, and alpha reader, Melissa DiRienzo, I owe you another huge thank you! You're like a one-woman cheering section. You make me believe I have a brilliant mind, and you keep me going when I get stuck or think I never should've started writing in the first place. I don't know what I'd do without you. Thank you for getting excited when I share my messy half-baked story ideas.

Mom, sorry for all those times I didn't appreciate you when I was a teenager. And thanks for still wanting to be my friend anyway. I don't know where I'd be today without your friendship and encouragement. Thank you for your enthusiasm about my writing and for all your feedback on this book.

Bree Babin, thank you for sharing all the crazy awkward situations you get yourself into and then allowing me to write a variation of those troubles. I speak on behalf of everyone when I say we appreciate you letting us share in your discomfort. Thanks for being my friend for the last and eighty-three years. (I hope I did the math correctly)

Leah Anastasakis, thank you for all your notes on this book. Your feedback was so incredibly helpful, and I'm grateful to have gained you as a beta reader.

To my father-in-law, Tim, thank you again for catching so many of those tiny details.

Thank you to my beta readers, Heather Mackenzie and Heather Coates for squeezing this book into your crazy schedules. I truly appreciate both of you.

To my husband, who inwardly groans when I give myself a tight deadline. Thank you for putting up with me when I've been writing for days and start skipping showers and meals. And thank you for feeding me when I'm hangry. You make this hangry unshowered woman very happy. Thank you for continuing to choose me. Forever and ever.

To my cheer section in the back, and anyone I missed, thank you!

SNEAK PEEK FROM PURPLE ROSES

TRAVIS

For Addison's twenty-third birthday, Addie, Oli, and I went out and celebrated like old times. There was a reason Addison and I were friends, aside from her being Oliver's girlfriend. She was smarter than she let on and more opinionated than she wanted anyone to know. She was witty with a dark humor she kept hidden. I thoroughly enjoyed picking on her with her type A personality that she tried desperately to keep under wraps. It was a trait she deemed less than perfect, and she airbrushed her imperfections, determined to conceal the characteristics she saw as flaws. But in doing so, the best parts of her dimmed. She was doing everyone a gross injustice but was too stubborn to see the truth.

I refused to let her pull that shit with me. I excelled at drawing out the real Addison. I knew exactly how to get under her skin. I drove her just crazy enough to get her to break the pretentious facade. I often wondered if Oliver ever questioned her little inconsistencies. Oliver wasn't an idiot, he had to notice the small changes in her, but ultimately I decided he didn't want to see them. He was stupid in love, insanely happy, and he'd always had an optimism that made him gloss right over those small things that should've made him ask deeper questions.

I could've popped their happy little bubble, but that felt unusually cruel, and despite all of Addison's pretenses, I knew how much she loved Oliver.

My dedication to seeing them happy together had me trying to liken Addison to something of a sister. I had to do something to lessen my attraction to her, but the moment she stepped out in her skimpy Little Red Riding hood costume, I knew that was a joke. My feelings toward her were far from familial, and the image of her in the scraps of red fabric and lace would forever be burned into my memory, filed away under the ever-growing Addison Arthur spank bank.

There wasn't a single bit of her that didn't tempt me, from her red *fuck-me* heels, which elongated her already long legs to her loose *just-been-fucked* blonde curls. A corset I was dying to unlace bound the sexy crimson dress, and the tiny mini skirt flared out in lace ruffles that barely covered her ass. I instantly had visions of bending her over the counter where she stood and taking her from behind. But the nail in my coffin was the diamond pattern thigh-high tights that ended halfway up her thighs. There was a good portion of smooth bare skin showing between the tights and skirt. That stretch of sensitive skin begged to be touched, preferably while her legs were wrapped over my shoulders, and I was tasting the sweet honey between her spread thighs.

She bit her lip as if she knew exactly what was going

through my mind, which she probably did as I couldn't fucking tear my eyes away from her, and I was growing rock solid in my pants. I shifted, trying to hide my reaction to her. And it couldn't have come a second too soon as Oliver stepped out in his Big Bad Wolf costume. It was basically a sleeveless hoodie with a faux fur hood that had wolf ears and matching furry fingerless gloves. His costume wasn't anything special, but it indicated to everyone that Addison belonged to him.

"Are you a cop or a stripper," Oliver asked, regarding my sleeveless police costume.

"Both," I said, twirling the plastic black baton. "The cuffs are real."

Addison accused, "You just wanted to show off your biceps."

I gave a cocky shrug. "Gotta show off my best assets, and I can't go with my dick out, so I had to settle for second best. But the pants tear away like stripper pants. Easy access."

"Just try to keep your pants on until you leave the party," Oliver noted.

"I can't promise anything. I might have to do a striptease just to take attention off Addison in that fucking scrap of a costume."

Oliver took his time looking over Addison. "I'm not sure how long we'll be at the party, anyway."

Travis laughed. "You're already coming in your pants, aren't you?"

PURPLE ROSES coming February, 2021

ALSO BY ANNA REZES

Pink Wine & Roses

~ VALLA SERIES ~

ABOUT THE AUTHOR

ANNA REZES has been passionate about writing since she was a child. When she's not busy honing her super-powers or traveling to other worlds full of fictional characters, she is spending time with family and friends. She lives in Ohio with her husband, their three dogs, and their sometimes cat.

...

For more from Anna Rezes visit:
www.annarezes.com
www.instagram.com/anna_rezes
www.facebook.com/annarezesauthor
amazon.com/author/annarezes
goodreads.com/author/show/19051292.Anna_Rezes

www.ingramcontent.com/pod-product-compliance
Lightning Source LLC
Chambersburg PA
CBHW021158130626
46554CB00005B/1878